BREAKING and ENTERING

Laura Semonche Jones

TIDAL PRESS

Copyright © 2011 Laura Semonche Jones
All rights reserved.

Published in the United States by Tidal Press.
Learn more at www.TidalPress.com.

These stories are works of fiction. Names, characters, places and incidents are either the product of the author's imagination or are used fictitiously. Any resemblance to actual locales or persons, living or dead, is entirely coincidental.

Cover photograph by Nicole Gagner.

ISBN: 0-9846617-0-0
ISBN-13: 978-0-9846617-0-1

To Rob.

*For being, for loving, for reading.
For everything.*

Always.

Even the reverse side has a reverse side.

Japanese proverb

CONTENTS

Acknowledgements	1
Breaking and Entering	5
Once Lucky, Twice Shy	21
March of Madness	39
Where Birds Go In a Hurricane	65
Fallout Shelter	81
Raw Materials	97
Instead	121
Border Crossing	125
Too Close for Comfort	139
Migration	149
The Arctic Swallow	163
About the author	*197*

ACKNOWLEDGMENTS

Thank you first to Tim Johnston and Short Story America for publishing *Fallout Shelter* at www.shortstoryamerica.com and including it in Short Story America's inaugural anthology. That honor encouraged me to forge ahead with this book. Thank you also to all my friends and family and teachers who were enthusiastic and supportive about this project from its infancy to its conclusion.

I owe a debt of gratitude to Joseph Morgenstern for his engrossing article, "The Fifty-Nine Story Crisis", which appeared in the May 29th, 1995 issue of *The New Yorker*. It stuck with me all these years and became the inspiration for my story, *Once Lucky, Twice Shy*.

Without the professional assistance of my friends John Grant and Stacey Evans on the design of the cover, I would have been lost. Speaking of the cover, I am grateful that artist Nicole Gagner was so gracious and generous in allowing me to use her photograph. That image haunted me from the moment I saw it, and it conveys everything I think these stories are about.

I write to process the world. I am interested in how people become who they are, how their choices and reactions to events over which they have no control affect their next choices and their next reactions, how their mistakes and successes and other people's mistakes and successes mix to form them, and how everything is connected, but rarely by the threads we think.

So to everyone who has ever listened to me talk about these things, especially my amazing and patient husband, thank you. To all the writers whose work has touched on these themes and transported me, thank you. To those people who put little perfect moments into the world that become the seeds of stories, thank you. You are all a part of this book. I hope you find yourself in its pages.

And to all the animals who have kept me company while I read and write, beginning with my childhood dog, Amy, thank you for providing furry encouragement and many opportunities to escape my head and go for a walk.

But without my parents, I would never have become a writer. Thank you most of all Mom and Dad.

*eleven
stories*

BREAKING AND ENTERING

By four o'clock in the afternoon the daylight was backing out of the room like a beaten dog. The only windows faced north or east so of all the places in the house, the end of the day always came first to their bedroom. The beginning too, but lately Bernie hasn't appreciated the dawn much; it just mocks him with promises it can't keep. Ever since he and Sophie made their decision, each day evaporated more quickly than usual even in the sunny rooms. And there was something else new too - a kind of violence in the way the days ended that startled him.

It was late November, a grim time to do anything, but it was the very grimness of the season that sucked out any strength he might have had left to resist her plan. On a sunny spring day, a man could have hope, and he could force it on his wife. It didn't help that it was cold, and not just outside. Bernie was still following Sophie's wishes and keeping the thermostat turned down low for Walter's sake. He had a thick undercoat, and she always worried about him being hot. Bernie did not want Sophie to worry.

He got up from the armchair by her bed. It used to be their bed of course, but he has been sleeping in the guest room, or on that chair, for the past few months. Out of habit he went to the bathroom to wash his hands.

The weather forecast called for thunderstorms later, which was unsettling for this time of year, although also a little comforting. Sophie always loved thunderstorms, even more once she got sick. "They are the only action I get," she would say. A couple of months ago, during one of the last big summer storms, she told Bernie that she liked to imagine lightning striking the house, then entering her body and re-animating her, like Dr. Frankenstein's monster. She had faked a seizure for effect and knocked over her IV stand. They laughed until they cried. Sophie hadn't said anything that funny or crazy in a long time. She hadn't spoken at all since Thursday. That was when she made him promise to go through with it on her birthday. Her birthday was yesterday, but Bernie just couldn't do it then, no matter what she wanted. It felt wrong, too symmetrical and neat. To be born and die on the same day wasn't natural. It smacked of a strange kind of luck, which he felt they hadn't had since Sophie got sick. And what was one more day? The living should get a say in the scheduling of death.

Back from the bathroom, Bernie put on his glasses and summoned what strength he had left. He turned on the light and opened the drawer of his wife's bedside table. He pulled out the box that held the equipment he needed and set it on the side of the bed. Then he slid the covers down at an angle and exposed just her left arm. He didn't want her to get cold. He got out the rubber tubing and tied it halfway between her left elbow and shoulder. She seemed to help him by lifting her arm a little. He held his breath and waited in case she might pull her arm back, in case she might somehow show him that she didn't want this anymore. But the arm did nothing. So he kept going, opening a new syringe and filling it from the bottles of morphine they had hoarded. He kissed her. Sophie fluttered her eyelids in what seemed like a response. Was she trying to say something? Should he wait? He waited, but there was nothing more. He sent a wordless prayer for her soul and his to a God he stopped believing in a long time ago but hoped was still there, waiting for Sophie. Then he found a vein, inserted the needle, closed his eyes and pushed the plunger. He knew that it was the right thing to do, but he felt sick.

Bernie had always followed Sophie's lead; it was in his nature to follow, and she was good at leading. She had been in horrible pain for months now, and at their last visit her doctor had said he didn't have any tools left in his toolbox. God, how Bernie hated that expression. He hated the doctor, too, partly for his poor choice of expressions but mostly for the fact that he couldn't save Sophie. Bernie looked at the clock. It had been forty seconds since he put the needle in her arm. The hospice nurse had said it would take less than a minute. This shouldn't be how someone dies, Bernie thought. You should get to say goodbye. When Sophie's chest rose for the last time with a little ragged gasp and then fell, when it clearly wasn't going to move again, the finality of what they had done – what he had done – overwhelmed him. He had killed her. She went limp, and he did too. He glanced briefly at Walter, but the dog hadn't moved. Bernie took off his glasses and buried his face in what little flesh the cancer had left. He waited to cry.

Walter showed up at their house twelve years ago, a rangy not-quite-puppy who introduced himself by knocking over their garbage can looking for food. The dog loved Sophie from the instant they met, her with a broom in her hands and him with his nose in a foil pie plate. At the time they had a cat who has long since died. The cat liked Walter, and Walter tolerated the cat the way an older brother allows a younger sibling to tag along, but never actually participate in any action. Bernie and Sophie would spend summer evenings on the deck with a cocktail watching the cat follow Walter around the yard, always staying about five feet away just in case. Their vet said he was probably a mix of German Shepherd and Alaskan Malamute and prone therefore to establishing a strong attachment to one person. In his prime, he was truly beautiful. He had a black face and huge brown body and a black tail that swooshed like a flamenco dancer's fan when he walked. And that undercoat that worried Sophie so much; it was almost white near his skin. He was getting old, though. The white recently spread to his muzzle, leaving him with salt and pepper fur around his nose and eyes. Worse, he has seemed half dead from grief for weeks now, as if he knew what was coming. But the fact that Walter hadn't intervened when Bernie killed Sophie made him feel marginally better about the whole horrible mess.

Bernie didn't know how long he had been kneeling at the bed waiting for the world to start again, his head on Sophie's stomach, one arm draped over her hip and one over her shoulder, but it was completely dark except for the glow of the bedside lamp when he heard the glass break. He pushed himself to his feet so he could go downstairs to investigate. That was usually Walter's self-appointed job, but since Sophie got sick, the dog hadn't left her side except to eat and take the two walks a day that Bernie had forced on him for both their sakes. And Walter showed no signs of getting up even though his ward was dead, his job over.

Bernie kicked off his slippers and slid his feet into his shoes. He figured the sound came from one of the lanterns that

Sophie bought for the porch last summer getting knocked over by the storm. He walked past the dog's bed which was under the biggest of the windows. "I guess it's just you and me, now, you sweet old boy. Thank you for being with her," Bernie said as he rubbed the dog's head.

Downstairs, he felt a rush of wind and saw that the kitchen door was open. When he went to shut it, he could feel that a single pane next to the doorknob was broken. Someone was in the house. On a different day, he would have been frightened, but not today. He longed for younger eyes for a moment – he was almost legally blind without his glasses - but then he realized he really didn't care what happened so what did it matter if he couldn't see it coming. He had faced his worst fear upstairs. Because he thought he should, he went to the living room and without turning on the light felt for and opened the fake edition of *Moby Dick*. It was the third book from the left on the third shelf from the top. He opened it and got the gun Sophie made him buy in case the morphine didn't work. How could the morphine not work, he had asked her. "I want a back up plan. Just get the gun, okay?" she had pleaded. And of course he had.

His footsteps apparently hadn't made enough noise, so he had the element of surprise on his side when he saw the man in his office. Bernie held the gun at his side, not bothering to aim it.

"What are you doing in here?" he asked the dark shape.

"Shit! Fuck man! No one was supposed to be here. Shit! Don't shoot!" The man turned out to be a kid and hopped in place like the floor was burning his feet.

"Well, I am here, and I'm not going to shoot unless I have to. What are you stealing?" Bernie had never been so unafraid or so calm in his life. It felt strangely good. And powerful.

"Nothing, man. Nothing. I was just looking for something that maybe..."

"That maybe you could sell for drugs?" Bernie Cohen hated to stereotype the young black man in his home, but the evidence seemed to point with a giant flashing yellow arrow to his conclusion.

"Nah, man. I don't do drugs." Gerard kept looking over his shoulder. Even with his bad eyes, Bernie could see he was looking for someone.

"Is someone waiting for you outside?"

"No. Yeah. Shit." The tempo of Gerard's high stepping increased.

"Are you sure you don't do drugs? You seem high." Bernie used to be a high school principal before he took early retirement twelve years ago. He knew what kids looked like high.

"Yeah, I'm sure. I'm not stupid. I'd know if I did drugs."

Bernie had to laugh. "Fair enough. Why are you here, then?"

Gerard didn't answer the question. Bernie waited.

"Look, I just need to get out of here."

Bernie felt brave so he raised the gun. "Give me back whatever you took."

"I didn't get nothing yet, man. You don't have anything nice."

Bernie laughed again. "No, I guess not."

"Sorry. I didn't mean to be rude..."

Bernie was taken aback by the kid's apology. "It's okay. Well, go then. And don't come back." Bernie lowered the gun, and the kid sprinted for the door and ran smack into a full grown version of himself.

"What the fuck are you doing taking so long?" the man asked Gerard.

"Dad, there's an old man. . ." Gerard pointed, and his father looked in the direction of his finger.

"Fuck!" Portis pulled out his own gun at practically the speed of light and aimed it at Bernie. "Get down motherfucker!"

Bernie got down.

"Drop your gun, old man."

Bernie dropped his gun.

"Push it over to me."

Bernie pushed the gun as hard as he could, but it didn't slide very far on the carpet. The only sound for a minute was everyone's breathing. Which was actually quite loud, Bernie thought.

"Dad, what are we going to do?"

"That's a good question," Bernie said. "What are we going to do?"

"Shut up! I'm trying to think," Portis answered.

"Don't hurt yourself," Bernie said, surprised by his cockiness under the circumstances.

"Shut up old man! Do you want me to shoot you?"

"Now that you mention it, I kind of do. That might be the solution."

"What the hell do you mean by that?" Portis yelled.

"Well, I just killed my wife, and I'm pretty sure I don't want to live without her."

"You what, asshole?"

"You thought you were the criminals here, didn't you? Well, have you ever murdered anyone? I have. If this is a contest, I think I win. Big. And I don't care what happens to me. So stop trying to scare me, you thug." Bernie gave this speech while still lying on the floor.

Portis didn't know what to do. In his line of work, he hadn't encountered victims who wanted to die. In fact, he tried to choose houses where he was sure he wouldn't run into any victims. Victims kind of took the fun out of burglary. But the old man didn't look like a murderer. He looked. . . Portis didn't know what he looked like.

"Get up."

Bernie got up. Portis looked at him for a long time.

"Dad?"

"This is some seriously weird shit," Portis said, shaking his head.

"Should we leave?" Gerard asked.

"No, we need to know what happened."

"Why?"

"Because now we're like the police here. This old man's confessed to us."

"Or you're like a couple of priests," Bernie said.

"What the fuck do you mean by that old man? You making fun of God?"

"My name's Bernie, not old man, and I just mean that priests hear confessions just like the police do, only they don't do anything about it other than forgive you."

"You want us to forgive you?" Portis asked.

"No, I don't. I was just making a point."

"What do you want us to do?" Gerard asked.

"Who cares what the old man wants?"

"Bernie," Bernie said.

"We're in charge here," Portis said. "I'll call you what I want to call you. Tell me what you did old man, and why you did it, and we'll decide what to do."

"I didn't know judgment day would come so soon."

"Well it did and we're here. What did you do? Wait, Gerard, get his gun."

Gerard picked up Bernie's gun from the floor and put it on the desk where Portis was sitting. Portis slipped it into the back of his jeans.

"I'll show you. Are you afraid of dogs?" Bernie asked.

"Why, you got a dog?" Portis said. "I don't hear no barking."

"Maybe he killed the dog too," Gerard said.

"I did not kill Walter. He has never hurt anyone, and I doubt he would hurt you even if you shot me. He was my wife's dog, body and soul. He is by her bed now. Upstairs."

"Well, fine, let's go upstairs. I ain't afraid of no dog anyway. Walk, old man."

"Bernie."

Portis poked the nose of his gun into Bernie's side and directed him upstairs. Gerard followed behind.

Walter lifted his head as they entered the bedroom, but didn't otherwise move. He had nothing left to protect. It wasn't that he didn't love Bernie and see him as his master, he was just empty, used up.

Portis walked over to Sophie's body and felt for a pulse in her exposed left wrist.

"You did kill her, man! Fuck you! That's wrong. That is so fucking wrong. Tell me why I shouldn't kill you for that," Portis turned the gun on Bernie.

"I don't really have a good reason, I guess."

"Why'd you kill her, man?"

"She begged me too."

"Why? Was she sick?" Gerard asked. Bernie turned around and realized Gerard was sitting on the floor petting Walter. Walter didn't seem to mind.

"She was terribly sick. She was dying, but too slowly for her taste. Sophie liked things to run on schedule, so she asked me to kill her, although that wasn't the word she used."

"So it was like assisted suicide? I've read about that," Gerard said.

"That was what she called it, and she wanted to die, but it doesn't matter what it is called. I killed her."

"So you're like some lame-ass Dr. Kevorkian?" Portis asked.

"Something like that."

Nobody said anything for a while. They just looked at Sophie.

"She looks peaceful. Was she in a lot of pain?" Portis lowered his gun.

"More than anyone should ever have to bear."

Gerard got up from Walter's side and they all stood in a semi-circle around Sophie's bed, looking at her.

"Well, Dad, I don't think he did anything wrong," Gerard said. "In school our teacher..."

"Don't let him off so easy. He may be lyin' through his teeth. He could think we're stupid. We don't have nothing but his word for it."

"Why would he lie to us?" Gerard said.

"I don't know. You ain't lyin' are you? Because even if we let you go, we know where you live. We find out that you're lyin'..."

"I'm not lying."

"I believe him, Dad."

"Fine. So you got all this life experience that means you can tell who are the good people and who are the bad?"

"I don't know. I just believe him," Gerard said.

Portis rolled his eyes and sighed. "Kids think they know everything. You got any kids?" he asked Bernie.

Bernie shook his head.

Portis waved the barrel of his gun toward Sophie's body. "How long was you two married?"

"Forty-three years. It was her birthday yesterday." Bernie started to cry for the first time. The numbness fell away like a coat sliding off his shoulders.

"Don't cry man," Portis said. "People get sick. People die. It's what happens. This is shit now, and shit that you had to help her die, but it's part of life. It's gonna be okay." He put his arm around Bernie's shaking shoulders.

Bernie let himself be hugged.

"Don't you need to call someone now?" Portis asked.

"I was going to, but then you broke in to my house. Why did you break into my house anyway?"

"The boy needs to learn the trade."

"Why my house?"

"No alarm, nice car, old people. And it's church supper night. All the old people around here go to the church tonight. And you all got something nice at home. We just steal stuff and sell it. We don't look to hurt people or kill them."

"Have you been to prison?" Bernie asked.

"I did two years inside 'bout ten years ago. But that was stupid. This is just a side job anyway. I'm going to open a barber shop with Gerard."

"Sounds like a good plan," Bernie said. "Everyone needs to get their hair cut. Is Gerard going to go to college, first? He should go to college."

"I'd like to go to college," Gerard said.

"You'll go to college, but we'll worry about that later," Portis said. "Bernie, you need to call someone and get her body treated with respect. We can't leave her here."

"We?"

"Yeah we, I'm involved now, ain't I?" Portis said.

"I guess so," Bernie said. He was glad to have the company, odd as it was. He got up to get the phone and the list of final instructions Sophie and he had worked out. He got his reading glasses too, even though they had written the list in big block letters. Sophie thought of everything.

"Who wrote that, man? A five year old?"

"I can't see very well."

"Ah, that sucks. My momma went blind before she died. Diabetes. What'd your wife have anyway?" Portis asked.

"Pancreatic cancer."

"How old was she?"

"62."

"That's not old."

"No, it isn't."

"How old are you?"

"73."

"Had yourself a hot young wife for a while, huh?" Portis elbowed Bernie in the side making him chuckle. He was very ticklish.

"I did, I guess. Sophie was very beautiful."

"Is that her in this picture?" Gerard asked, holding up the one of Sophie on a horse from college.

"Yeah. She had just come back from a camping trip."

"With horses?"

"Yeah."

"Wow. That sounds like fun," said Gerard.

"You ain't never been on a horse," said Portis. "How would you know that was fun?"

"I don't know, it looks like fun. And I like animals."

"Hmph. Well we gotta get going on this list. Let me see it." Portis decided the situation no longer required being armed, so he set his gun down on the dresser and was trying to pull Bernie's gun out of his belt when it fired.

"Jesus fucking Christ. Your gun shot me!" yelled Portis, dropping the gun. "Oh fuck, that hurts!"

Walter bolted out of the room, Bernie crumpled on the floor from the shock and the noise, and Gerard ran to his father's bleeding butt.

"It's okay Dad, it just grazed your skin. The shot went straight down, not into you."

"Shit it hurts!"

"I'm so sorry," Bernie said. "What can I do?" Bernie reached for the gun on the floor.

"Don't touch that!"

Bernie recoiled.

"Can I get a towel or a sheet or something?" Gerard asked Bernie.

In a panic, Bernie pulled the sheet off Sophie's body and Gerard fashioned a kind of diaper for his father to absorb the blood.

Then Bernie's phone started to ring.

"Don't answer that!" Portis yelled.

"It's probably my neighbor. She heard the shot."

"Do not answer it."

Bernie stayed where he was and the answering machine picked up.

"Bernie? Are you okay? I heard a noise. Are you there? Look, pick up the phone. Bernie, don't avoid me, pick up the phone. . ."

"She always treat you like a child, Bernie?" Portis asked, holding his butt.

Bernie laughed. "She does, kind of."

"I'm calling the police," she said and hung up.

"Oh shit," said Gerard.

"Don't worry," Bernie said. "Just hide, and I'll tell them to go away."

"Seriously?" Gerard asked. "You'd do that for us after we broke in your house?"

"He shot me!" Portis screamed.

"I did not shoot you. You shot yourself."

"With your crappy gun," Portis said, pouting.

"Where should we hide?" Gerard took charge.

"In the basement. Follow me." Bernie picked his gun up from the floor and tucked Portis' gun into the top drawer of the dresser and led them down to the basement.

"This is nice," Portis said, looking around. "I don't want to get blood on your carpet."

"Don't worry about any blood. And we finished it three years ago, just before Sophie got sick. She thought it would help with the sale. Just go in the closet here, and I'll come get you when they are gone." Bernie opened the door to a closet filled with Christmas decorations and beach chairs.

"Why the closet?"

"In case they insist on looking around."

"Okay. Don't take too long. I'm a little claustrophobic, man," Portis said.

"I'll hurry."

"Bring a beer when you get back, then we gonna tackle that list," Portis called through the door.

Bernie smiled and went back upstairs. He needed to come up with a plausible story for the shot. He would tell them he was cleaning the gun, or maybe checking to see if it was loaded. But why? Maybe they wouldn't ask any questions once they saw he was all right. He closed the basement door just as the sirens came up the street. He turned on the porch light and waited by the front door. He hoped they wouldn't see the broken kitchen door. There was no time to come up with a story for that, too. He looked next door and saw that Linda had pulled her curtains back and was watching the street. Two police cruisers came, and four officers got out.

Two went to his neighbor's house and two started up his front walk.

"Mr. Cohen?" they called out in booming but concerned voices. "It's the police. Are you all right? Can you open the door and come outside? We have a report of shots being fired."

A shot Bernie thought. One shot. Linda had exaggerated as always. He opened the door and was temporarily blinded by their flashlights. He raised his hand – the one with the gun still in it – to shade his eyes. For eyes that couldn't see very well, they were terribly sensitive to light.

"Put the gun down sir. Put it down now!" The voices changed.

Gun? Bernie forgot he had it in his hand. The light was doing something to his brain. He couldn't move. But they'll know I'm not going to hurt them, he thought.

"Mr. Cohen, put the gun on the ground and put your hands up!"

Even if he could have, they didn't give him a chance. Officer Kepper fired two shots. One right after the other. Both hit Bernie in the forehead, and he dropped, spilling two small streams of blood from two huge holes.

"Shit, we need an ambulance. Now!" Kepper shouted into his radio. "I was trying to hit his arm, to knock the gun out of his hand. Jesus Christ!" Kepper ran to the porch and tried to shake Bernie back to life.

In the basement, Portis and Gerard froze, afraid to speak.

"Kepper! Stop it. You're messing with the scene. Get a grip. He had a gun. You're okay. You did the right thing. We'll write it up right."

Officer Gomez pulled Kepper off of Bernie and sat him in the porch swing. It was only Kepper's second day on the force.

Linda came running over and pushed past Gomez. "Where's Sophie, you fool?" she shouted to Bernie's dead body.

"Who's Sophie?" Gomez asked.

"Sophie is his wife. She was sick, she must be. . ."

Gomez stopped listening and ran into the house. He checked the kitchen and living room and the office, and then he took the stairs two by two. He nearly crashed into Walter halfway up as the big dog flew down the stairs and out the open front door. He settled into a trot once he got far enough away from the house, his tail swishing like a metronome. Gomez made quick laps of the two guest bedrooms and the hall bathroom before he got to the master bedroom at the end of the hall.

"Holy fucking Jesus," he said when he saw Sophie and Portis' blood on the floor. Gomez stepped back and crossed himself. He pressed the button on his radio: "Derek, I've got another body here. We need backup."

ONCE LUCKY, TWICE SHY

"Sidney! There you are! I was frantic I wouldn't find you in this crowd." He stopped and put his hands on his knees and panted for a moment. "I would just die if I couldn't personally offer you my heartfelt congratulations on your amazing success." The short, balding man who grabbed her left hand while he was still a little bent over and pumped it furiously with both of his looked vaguely familiar. He also looked like he would have grabbed and shaken both of her hands, creating a four fisted bouncing ball of flesh, if her right hadn't been occupied with a flute of champagne.

Sidney was proud that she only flinched a little at his enthusiasm. Touching so many strangers left her feeling shrunken, and she wasn't used to the spotlight. She couldn't exactly unbuild her building now, though. And she did like the champagne.

"What a wonderful structure, truly breathtaking," he said, still out of breath with the effort of his search. "Such a brilliant design. You've made steel and glass sensuous and even soft. The building is a tribute to nature. To women! Kudos to you and your team. I can't wait to see what you do next. I do hope you'll stay in the country and not go off to work in Dubai or

China where all the rest of our brilliant architects have disappeared to." He disengaged his right hand and wagged a finger at her in a mock scolding. "We need you! And we love you. This building just changes absolutely everything. You know that don't you? Of course you do. Now I must get another drink. Be well and thank you!" He released her hand after giving it one last squeeze and headed into the belly of the crowd, waving over his shoulder before pulling out a handkerchief from the pocket of his child-sized tuxedo jacket and mopping the sweat off his forehead.

The skyscraper Sidney designed for Datrix Systems's headquarters was her masterwork. Sixty stories on curved stilts, with a hollow core. Green glass for the windows and blue stone for the walls. It looked like Neptune's spaceship one reviewer said, not minding, apparently, that Neptune was god of the sea, not air. Jack loved it, too, which mattered more than Sidney cared to admit. A few reviewers called it The Jellyfish, but no one doubted its technical virtuosity and originality. And that was precisely what Datrix Systems wanted – a building that would echo the company's vision of itself as an innovator. They wanted a building that was all about art and communication and risk taking. Sidney's original design changed little in the building process. It sprang from her brain one night at 2am and felt mythological to her, almost pre-ordained.

"Are you ready for a night of that?" Jack cocked his elbow in the direction of the retreating man. "I think he was clearly in love with you."

"It was a little over the top. Who was he anyway?" Sidney took a sip of her champagne as a sort of palate cleanser.

"A devoted fan. Remember your picture has been in the paper several times, easy for architecture groupies to cut out and tape to their walls and make googly eyes at. 'Sidney Reed, savior of the art of American architecture!' There will undoubtedly be proclamations and probably statues in your future."

Sidney laughed and played along. "Where's my sword? I'm sure there will be beasts and villains to fight. I'll need a fine weapon if I am to be a good savior. Medieval and encrusted with jewels please." She performed a mini curtsey and with a flourish of her arm, offered her palm. Jack placed an imaginary sword in it with equal flourish.

He was pleased to see his wife having a little fun with the evening and her fame. He was worried that she would feel unworthy. But last time wasn't really her fault at all. The clients were crazy, and the engineers lied. It was sad and wasteful that the Trevant Technologies tower had to be torn down a year after it was completed, but it was in no way her fault. Everyone who mattered knew she wasn't responsible. But the experience shattered Sidney and stole three years of their marriage while Sidney's doctors tinkered with medication to help her get her emotional equilibrium back.

Now she was back and off the meds, but Jack knew Sidney was still fragile, one piece of bad news away from a breakdown. All artists are a little fragile; they have to be in order to process the world. Or at least that was how he saw it. But keeping Sidney safe and healthy for both their sakes was his responsibility. Jack had been able to retire two years ago and since he didn't like golf, he spent a lot of time worrying about and supporting Sidney. It was worth it, not just because he loved her, but because she was good. He felt his contribution to society was keeping her fit enough to make more beautiful things. He tried not to let Sidney go to that part of town to see the gaping hole in the earth where the tower had been, afraid she would get sucked back into the void. It had to be enough that this new building was sound and beautiful and on the cover of magazines. The president and CEO of Datrix Systems were thrilled with their building, the other tenants were happy, and the city was happy. Sidney had hit the trifecta, but she seemed on the edge of thinking she didn't deserve it. Jack figured the memory of that damn tower pecked away at her confidence. She exhausted herself on this project triple checking everything too, and Jack was worried about her physical health if she didn't get some rest soon.

"Maybe we can use that sword to raid a castle or two when we get to Portugal," Jack checked his watch "just 36 hours from now. We could even re-use those stockings," Jack pointed at her legs. "I know how much you hate wearing them."

"They make my legs itch. And we need to think about giving away some of this money, not looking for more."

"True, true. We are pretty comfortable now, thanks to you. Do you want to set up a foundation?"

"That sounds lovely. We'll have to write up a mission statement before we do anything else. Maybe we can get started on that in Portugal?"

"Darling, Portugal is for vacation. Remember what that is? No, you don't. Mrs. Silva and I will have to re-educate you about the meaning of that word. We can work on the foundation when we get back."

"Okay, okay. Only wine and sun and food in Portugal."

"And sex." Jack winked at her.

"Oh, that sounds like fun! I'm sorry I've been so busy and tired. I'll make it up to you."

"That is a deal."

Both Jack and Sidney still felt lucky to have found each other. When they met, Jack was running a residential construction company in New Jersey. Sidney was an architecture student. They instantly disliked each other, based solely on their occupations. But a mutual friend kept throwing them together, and Jack discovered that Sidney wasn't stuck up or impractical, just thoughtful and desperately artistic. She knew math as well as design and could also swing a hammer with the best of them. Eventually Sidney realized Jack wasn't a dumb jock only looking to make money by throwing up McMansions on treeless lots. He did all of his own design and treated his employees fairly. So they were not such an odd match. That was over twenty years ago.

"It's not just the itchy stockings, my feet hurt, too." Sidney kicked out of one slingback for a moment and kneaded her toes on the plush burgundy carpet.

"I told you not to wear heels. You're an artist, not a fashion model, although you do look especially lovely, my dear." Her husband kissed her cheek. "And those feet will recover nicely in the sand. You just have to survive one dinner in your honor. You can do it. Come on." Jack offered his arm, which Sidney obediently took.

"I guess I can make it to the table. I'm starved, too. Oh wait, you have my phone, don't you?" Sidney said, disengaging and looking panicked.

"Yes, darling. Right here." He patted his chest pocket. The tiny phone wouldn't fit inside Sidney's tiny beaded bag. Sidney visibly relaxed and reconnected. She'd been so tied to her phone for the building process, she was having a hard time breaking the habit of carrying it everywhere and worrying when she didn't have it. But now she really could toss it in the river if she wanted to. She had no new project lined up, even though everyone was clamoring to hire her.

Sidney slid her shoes back on and took a deep breath and a moment to absorb the flowers, the lights, the tuxedos and gowns, and the music from the two jazz trios. Servers were circulating like dancers with carefully constructed canapés on trays draped with gold linen. It was too much, yet it was what she always wanted. Datrix Systems had spared no expense on this party.

"Thank you," she said to Jack, hugging his arm.

"For what? I had nothing to do with this. This is all you."

"No, I wouldn't have been able to do any of this without you."

"That's bullshit and you know it. I just held down the home front, fed the dog and took you out to dinner when I could pry you away."

"Nope." Sidney shook her head with teenage defiance. "You and I both know it's more than that."

"I won't let you diminish what you did," Jack said matching her defiance with equal firmness. "You are amazing. You built the most unique and beautiful skyscraper in the world. Tonight is about that. About you, my wonderful wife." He spun her around and kissed her hard on the mouth. "I love you more than you'll ever know, and I am amazed by you."

Sidney kissed him back with equal fervor.

"Hey break it up you two," shouted Louis, one of the engineers on the Datrix Systems project, as he walked over. "Or get a room. Although it is good to see the boss let her hair down." A chunk of Sidney's blonde hair had escaped during their embrace. She pushed it behind her ear and blushed.

"Good to see you man," Jack said patting Louis on the back. "Enjoying the party?" Jack always could recover his composure quickly. He kept a proprietary hand on Sidney's back.

"You bet. This is amazing. I hope I'm not intruding, but I came alone..."

"Not at all Louis," Sidney said. "It is good to see you here. You deserve a huge part of the credit and it was great fun to work with you, except when you wouldn't let me add the arches," she playfully nudged his arm.

"They couldn't carry the load, but I agree they would have been lovely. Maybe another project."

"Yes hopefully another project."

"Don't forget you got a lot of innovative ideas into this one. The base on stilts for one. No one thought that could be done safely. And it makes the building float so beautifully."

"Good point. I'm being greedy." She hugged both men.

"Look, there are Vernon and Phil," Jack said

"Oh, I'd like to talk to them. Let's go over." The president and vice-president of Datrix Systems waved as they saw Sidney approaching.

"This night is stupendous. What a party. Everyone is here. We've gotten amazing press, the community is happy with the design and then to have the building get the AIA award is the icing on the cake. Congratulations to all of us," Vernon raised his glass and received enthusiastic clinks in response.

They chatted for a while before Vernon and Phil were pulled away by their wives to dance. Louis, Jack and Sidney watched the slide show of the construction process that ran continuously over both bars. Louis and Sidney were in almost every shot.

"I'm going to head to the restroom and freshen up before we're seated for dinner," Sidney said.

"Okay. I'll be right here. Come get me and we'll head to the table. Don't get waylaid. I'm sure there are admirers lurking in the corners, ready to whisk my fair lady away."

Sidney laughed and waved him off.

Jack watched her still shapely rear end encased in the lavender beaded gown until she was swallowed by the crowd. Jack had to persuade her to buy that dress. She was normally more comfortable in job site clothes – jeans and untucked shirts. But this gown showed off her flawless skin and dancer's body, and tonight she needed movie star clothes. He was relieved this award had come to Sidney. She had never found the right people to work with, the right team, until now, just shy of her 50th birthday. A good age to reach the pinnacle, he realized. Not too young where a fall has to be in your future and not too old that people don't take you seriously. Architecture, unlike other creative fields, demands some physical vigor.

The buzzing in his pocket interrupted his happy thoughts. Louis excused himself and unthinking, Jack answered Sidney's phone. It was Eric, one of Sidney's assistants who should have been at the party.

"Um, hi Jack. Can I talk to Sidney?"

"She's busy right now. What do you need her for? Shouldn't you be here?" Jack didn't like Eric. Sidney had spent many evening hours complaining about his work. Jack encouraged Sidney to fire him, but Sidney just hoped she could turn him around.

"I really need to talk to her. It's about the building."

"What about it? Tell me and I'll tell her."

"Uh, she's not going to be happy..."

Jack snorted with laughter. He'd had just enough to drink to be a little mean. "Nothing you can say will make her unhappy Eric. You don't have that kind of power, not tonight."

"Oh yeah? Well, I think I do. I think she'll be pretty unhappy when you tell her I discovered a flaw with the building. It won't handle quartering winds from the north, you know, winds coming on a diagonal that hit two sides of a building at once."

"I know what quartering winds are, you arrogant jackass."

"Well, the supports and her bracing system made the building particularly vulnerable to quartering winds over 100mph coming from the north."

"A big storm isn't going to come from the north, not the way the weather patterns run on the east coast."

"So? She's still going to have to go public, fix the problem. The engineers used welds and not the bolts she wanted, so she needs to..."

"She needs to do nothing. How did you find out about this?"

"I was doodling around..."

"Looking for some way to take your boss down and grab some glory?

"No, I just was curious since the storm is coming."

"Hurricane Felix is coming from the south."

"Hurricanes rotate, and she can't take the chance. She'll need to tell Datrix Systems and get started on a fix and evacuate the building. That's what I would do."

"Bullshit. You don't know what you are talking about." Jack saw Sidney in the crowd. "Look, I'll call you back," he said firmly and clicked the phone shut.

Sidney returned from the restroom into the crush of the party glowing even more than before. "I passed a replica of my building on the way back," she told Jack as she squeezed the arm he offered her. "My first thought was 'that's gorgeous, who did that?' Then I realized it was mine. My building. I finally have my building. I am so happy."

Jack kept his rising panic to himself during dinner. So Eric said he had found a flaw in the stilt design. Sidney often complained about Eric's work, so it seemed unlikely he was suddenly a genius and had found some flaw no one else had seen. Plus Jack had never liked Eric as a man. But what if he was right? Jack didn't know how to tell, but he knew he had to keep Eric from telling Sidney anything. Facing Eric's claims would shatter her, and he would not let that happen. He would face it for her.

The rest of the evening passed in a blur for both of them, but for very different reasons. Jack excused himself before dessert, grateful for the cover smoking gave him. Sidney frowned a little in disapproval, but no more than usual. He had trouble finding a balcony with no one else nearby but finally did and called Eric back.

"Look, I know why you are doing this," Jack hissed.

"Yeah, to try and fix the building and maybe save some lives."

"No, Mr. Hotshot, you're doing this to further your own career. You can't make it by yourself, so you're going to be the giant slayer, rising to fame by taking someone else down. I won't let you do that to Sidney. The likelihood of what you say might happen is so slim that it is almost non-existent. But you'd be the hero once the media got a hold of it, and Sidney would be destroyed."

Eric sighed in the face of Jack's attacks. "Quartering winds do happen, they will happen, maybe with the arrival of Hurricane Felix, and the building will not withstand them if they are over 100 mph. I ran the models. The braces for the stilts are elegant, but insufficiently strong. If those winds happen, there is about a 1 in 10,000 risk it could collapse. If you think Sidney can live with that and all those dead people, fine."

"Dozens of engineers passed this project," Jack continued. "It meets the standards; everything is to code. It is safe as it needs to be. As it could be," he corrected himself.

"Sure, it meets all standards, but I found a flaw. Someone else will too. And so will the hurricane. I can't turn my back on it."

Jack was getting confused. Sidney had been lied to by engineers before and didn't see it. Maybe. . .

"So it's all about trust and doing the right thing and not your pocketbook? I think you're jealous," Jack spat at him, trying to buy time.

"Look, if something happens any investigation will find the cause. And it would be easy to fix now. The braces just need to be reinforced with bolts to withstand the transfer of motion by the stilts. It will be messy and expensive, but doable. If I were Sidney, I'd want to fix it. Her reputation will be even stronger. I don't understand why you guys are fighting me on this."

"Who else knows?"

"No one," Eric said without thinking. "I called as soon as I was sure. I'm at the office now."

Jack decided to go with threats. "If you were Sidney, there would be no building. There is a lot you don't understand. But I think you'll understand this. I will ruin you if you say anything. I have people who can find out a few things you don't want public if you even think about saying anything to anyone else. And those same people can do other things you won't like."

Jack rarely brought up, or thought about, his old friends in Jersey City. But he knew they would still do anything for him.

"Fine, geesh. You are a cold asshole. But don't think it will be on me when that building comes down."

"It is not going down, you are."

Jack flipped the phone shut, thought a moment, and re-opened it. He didn't know if Morris was still at his old number, but he had to try before Eric had time to change his mind and spread the news of his discovery.

He answered on the third ring.

"'Lo?"

"Morris, it's Jack."

"Holy fuck! I thought you was dead! How are you?"

"I'm great Morris, but I need a favor."

"If you need a favor from me, you ain't great."

"Okay, not so great right now. But great before today, and I'll be great again. How are you?" Jack remembered to ask.

"I'm all right. Hip's giving me trouble and so is the missus, but I've got a new 50 inch 3D flat screen for the games, so life is good. What do you need?"

"You still in the business?"

"Yeah. Sometimes."

"If I give you a name and an address, can you help me out?"

"Nope."

"Why not? You just implied you were still in the business."

"But you're not. You calling me out of the blue, how do I know it's not a set-up?"

"I wouldn't do that to you."

"Fine. Agreed. But you're too emotional. I can tell it in your voice. Think about it and call me back in a week."

"I don't have a week. Sidney doesn't have a week."

"Is she sick? Ah, Jack. . ."

"No she's not sick. This guy is just out to destroy her reputation."

"Ah, now that she's famous. People survive that stuff. It's not worth killing for. No, Jack, I can't stick my neck out for you on that. Go figure something else out, but don't be stupid. Promise me."

Jack didn't say anything.

"Ah jeez. Call me back in a week. Don't do anything stupid for a week okay?"

"Bye Morris. Take care of that hip."

Jack closed the phone and walked back to dinner, composing his face and his posture as he went. He kissed

Sidney when he returned, but she barely noticed. She was happily drunk and giddy with pleasure. He wouldn't let anything spoil that. He'd figure something out.

Jack and Sidney took a cab home once they extricated themselves from the last of the well wishers. Sidney fell asleep instantly, but Jack lay there, trying to decide if Eric would keep quiet, if he had done enough.

The next morning they watched the weather channel in nearly matching sweatpants and t-shirts and nursed their hangovers with coffee and aspirin. They saw that Hurricane Felix was heading straight for New York. It was an actual problem now, not a theoretical one. Jack had to increase the portion of his brain devoted to staying calm.

Sidney got up and turned off the television. "It looks like Felix is moving slowly enough we'll be able to get our flight, thank God. I am as excited about this trip as I have ever been. I think for once I can truly relax." She paused. "You look worried, what's wrong?"

"Do I? It's just my headache. It's been a while since I've had a hangover. I'll be fine, though. We have three hours before the car will come to take us to JFK. Do you want to get something to eat?"

"We probably should. I don't think I can do much more than toast, though."

"Okay. Let's head to Annie's on 13th."

"Sounds great. Did you remember to stop the mail?"

"Yup. And Roger is coming by once to water the plants. All taken care of, my lady," Jack bowed low to Sidney's sparkling laugh.

"It's amazing how easy it really is to pick up and go somewhere for two weeks. I always want to make it harder than it is," Sidney said as she pulled her hair into a low ponytail. "I must look like a bag lady. Let me change into some jeans. I'll be ready in a flash."

They walked to Annie's under cloudy skies that looked to contain no more than a few fall showers. Growing up in South Carolina, Jack felt he knew weather. He was sure this was no hurricane weather. He started to feel better. Even if Eric were right, the weather had to prove it. And he trusted his own gut over the Weather Channel's histrionics. At Annie's, they ate their way clear of the lingering effects of last night's champagne and wine and then got back to their apartment with enough time to shower and double check that they had something to read for the flight. The car arrived a little early, but they were both ready.

As they were getting in, Sidney's phone rang and Jack's stomach seized. He forgot to get rid of the phone. Something felt like it exploded in his head with a bright white flash. It's all going to come apart, he realized. The whole past three years. It was all he could do to breathe. He broke out in a prickly sweat.

Sidney fished it out of her purse, oblivious to Jack's rising panic. "Hello?"

"Sidney, it's Louis. I'm sorry to bother you as you are leaving, but I knew you'd want to know."

"About what?" Sidney didn't like what she heard in Louis' voice.

"Eric called me and said he thinks there is a problem with the building." Louis outlined what Eric told Jack.

Sidney sat down on the steps of their building, lost to Jack. "Well shit. That's not true. Let me think what's the best thing to do here."

"There's something else that Eric is claiming," Louis said, and he told her about Jack's threats.

It would be just like last time, Jack thought. He told the driver they wouldn't be needing him. It was all over. His vision started to get blurry. He pulled the bags out of the trunk and sat next to Sidney. He should have done more when he had the chance, he thought, should have gone to Eric's last night and made him disappear. He never should have waited, never should have hoped. Being so out of practice, that was the problem. Now there would be no vacation, no more celebration, no more feeling good. He had failed her and he felt sick. He steeled himself to help her put the pieces back together.

"Okay," Sidney said into the phone. "Meet me at the office in an hour. He's wrong, and I can explain it better there." She closed the phone and turned to Jack in a fury. "You knew? And your plan was to terrify him into keeping quiet? Who are you?"

Jack hadn't expected anger. "I didn't think you would survive another. . ."

"Seriously? Jesus, Jack. What kind of solution did you think that would be?"

"I was trying to protect you. To help. That's all I've been doing for years. Helping you. After last time. . ."

"Last time nearly killed me, but I learned from my mistakes. People change Jack. And I am a good architect. How could you not believe that, at least, even if you did think I was going to lose my shit? How could you not give me a chance to fix my own problems? How dare you take that away from me?"

"I was protecting you. I was helping you," Jack would repeat it until she understood. Maybe he'd gone about it the wrong way, but couldn't she see he loved her? "People who love each other do that."

Sidney stared at him. "Not like this. This is not love. What if I was wrong? What if the building was dangerous and people could die? You'd kill Eric to cover it up? I don't want that kind of love. That is sick. I never asked for that." Her hands were on her hips and hatred burned in her eyes.

Jack stared at her. The rejection made more explosions in his head.

"You have gotten confused." She turned to walk up the steps, then came back for her bags. "Our vacation is more important than my work, is that it? Eric just wanted to talk to me. I could have fixed this during the party if you had told me. Why did you lie to me?"

Jack was confused. Her face was so close to his, but it was so foreign, so twisted. He didn't remember the last time she was mad at him, if ever. Couldn't she thank him for his good intentions? What he was willing to do for her? Why did she take Eric's side? Why didn't she see he did what he did out of love? He had been doing everything out of love and she had taken it gratefully, greedily even. Why was this any different?

"Find somewhere else to stay tonight, please," Sidney said as she heaved her bags and headed up the stairs.

Jack took the stairs two at a time and grabbed her shoulder and spun her around.

"What the hell?"

He pushed her, and she nearly fell.

"Jack, stop it. I'm sorry. I . . " She looked scared, and it felt good to see the anger off her face.

He pushed her again. She stumbled forward and put her hands down on the top step. People started staring.

"Stop. Please. You're scaring me."

He had finished pushing her up the steps and decided to push her down. She lost her balance and fell backwards. Her bags cushioned her fall, but he heard something pop. The momentum of the fall carried her feet over her head and they kissed the ground and then kind of rolled to the side.

At least she stopped yelling at him.

"Jack, can you help me? I think my arm is broken, I . . ."

He sat down on the top step. Someone else could call an ambulance.

MARCH OF MADNESS

The morning at the store was terrible, and it sent Dave's hopeful mood spiraling back down to its usual spot in the basement of his soul. He was working with a couple who didn't speak English very well. They were from some Muslim or Arab country; the woman wore a veil. He tried to find out what they both wanted, but the husband kept yelling at Dave that he had to talk only to him and to stop staring at his wife. In this country, Dave wanted to say, the wives make the decisions about carpet and about anything that goes in the house. I was just playing by the rules, he wanted to say. But they walked out in a burst of what had to have been curses, and the boss signed him up for cultural sensitivity training. This community and the world are changing, his boss said, and we need to make sure we change with them. This is for your own good.

The day was supposed to go better than this. Dave – he had always gone by David until he started using the nickname last year in the hope that it would make him seem friendlier which would, he also hoped, lead to more sales – had followed his new morning routine perfectly for the very first time. So the day owed him; he had done his part, and life needed to start playing fair. He had gotten up fifteen minutes earlier than usual and done 50 situps and 50 pushups, most of which were knee push-ups like a girl would do, but he figured they counted. Then as suggested by his therapist, he wrote in his journal and made a list of things he wanted to accomplish and things he wanted to feel. He ate oatmeal for breakfast and put his dishes in the dishwasher so he wouldn't come home to another chore, however minor. Organization and staying on top of things are more important to mental health than we think, according to his therapist. Make the little stuff go smoothly and save your energy and emotional resources for the big stuff, she had said.

Fine. So now the day fucking owed him.

Whoa. Calm down, he thought. Calm. Down. He heard her voice again. "Things in life don't work so mathematically, Dave," when he asked when he would see results. As if he, of all people, didn't know that. "Good things will eventually come from good habits," she continued. Now that he needed to believe. Okay, forget the morning, he told himself. He could start the day over since he was on his way to his favorite part of the job. Pleased with his new resiliency, a trait he had learned after weeks of therapy was extremely important to develop, Dave walked to his car, sat in the driver's seat and rested his head on the headrest. He inhaled and exhaled slowly ten times. Then ten more. It was working. The breathing took forever and he was already running late, but it was really working. He kept up the exercise until he felt sufficiently in control to drive and face whatever new assault the world would hurl at him.

David Adams loved carpet. And he wasn't a snob. He loved the cheap shags and expensive berbers alike. Sometimes the smell of the cheap ones got to him, but still, he loved them. He loved the rolls they came on and he loved what new carpet represented: a clean slate, a new beginning, hope and change. But he hated working at The Carpet Palace, mostly because of the customers and partly because of his boss. He successfully ignored his co-workers without them knowing it. It was a skill he had honed since childhood. He felt they were unworthy, that none of them loved or even understood carpet like David did. David worked on commission, but he also got a decent base salary – everyone did – which he knew was rare in the business. So he stayed on.

But David – Dave – was tired. His wife left him last fall, and he hadn't seen their daughter since then. It wasn't his wife's fault, he had to admit. Short of driving Rachel over and throwing her out of the car, Abby had done everything she could to get them together. No, she was a fucking saint. Stop, he thought. His therapist told him that every time he even thought a curse word, much less spoke one, he was "elevating his anger." He had heard the phrase first as "elevatoring" his anger. The fake word made him laugh. Now every time he felt himself getting angry, he pictured an elevator flying toward the top floor with that little cartoon character with the guns and puffs of steam coming out of his ears. Pistol Pete or Yosemite Sam or somebody like that.

Dave had always thought in pictures. Words were hard for him. They would get jumbled. So he liked going to people's houses to measure; that was the easiest and best part of the job for him. He liked drawing out the space in his notebook, calculating the exact amount needed so there would be a little left over for an entry rug in the basement, or for the owners to use to pad something. He saw someone once use the extra carpet under a dog's crate to raise it off the floor. He always tried to imagine the lives people lived in the houses he visited. Each trip was like a vacation that way. For forty five minutes, he stopped living his life and lived theirs. Some of the other salesmen didn't like going to people's houses. They just wanted to stay in the store and rack up the numbers.

He got to the Channing house before he had finished his thoughts. He got out and rang the doorbell and by habit stood back so whoever answered could see him through the window next to the door. No one liked to open the door to someone they couldn't see, not even if they were expecting him. It didn't help that Dave was tall, six foot five last time he checked, which was probably ten years ago. But he hadn't shrunk; he wasn't that old yet, even if some mornings he felt like it. He did slouch though, as much from lack of exercise as trying to appear smaller.

He waited, then rang the doorbell again. He heard it ding-donging in the house, so he knew it worked. Still, he knocked for good measure. And waited some more. It was hot on the stoop, and clearly no one was coming. He had wasted his time. This happened about one out of every five trips. The people decided they didn't want new carpet, and they were too chicken or lazy to call and cancel the appointment. Dave thought maybe they should charge a fee or a deposit for the measuring, nothing big, just an amount large enough to make people bother to call and cancel to get their deposit back. His boss said no way.

Dave was going to go back to his car when he realized the thumping he was hearing was not someone's stereo but instead came from this house's backyard. Someone was home. So he walked to the side of the house and stuck his head around the corner. He saw a girl shooting baskets.

"Hi," Dave said, after she made one. "Is your mother home?"

Dave braced himself for an unpleasant reaction.

"Nope," the girl said, heaving up the ball. The basket was a full ten feet high, Dave figured, or at least pretty damn close to regulation height. And she was little. Her style wasn't pretty, but the ball swished through the net with that magical sound.

"Any adult? A babysitter, your father? Grandmother, aunt, uncle, neighbor? Nanny?"

He was trying to make the girl laugh. He knew she wouldn't have a nanny. Not in this neighborhood.

"Nope. Just me. And I'm not supposed to talk to strangers." She heaved the ball up again. Swish.

"Of course you're not. But your mother was expecting me. I'm here to measure your living room for new carpet."

"Oh." The girl put the ball down and ran inside and ran back out before Dave had a chance to react. He was never fast.

"Mom gave me this to give you. She measured it herself."

"Oh, that's nice of her, but I always need to do it too."

"Why?"

"Well, it's my job."

"But now you have the day off! Isn't that better?"

Look. Set. Heave. Swish. He wondered if basketball was a phase, or if she would go on to play in college.

"Not really. I could get in trouble."

"I'd get in more trouble if I let you in the house."

Fair enough, Dave thought and almost laughed. He persevered. "I need to do things like count doorways, see what kind of transitions we'll need. I need to see if there are any closets, or radiators, if you've got baseboard heating, all that stuff. Sometimes I have to cut a little piece of the old carpet away from the wall so I can see what the subfloor is made of." Dave patted the knife in the breast pocket of his shirt. "I've got to tell the installers what to expect. All of that is in addition to getting accurate measurements, which I am sure your mom did."

Swish. The girl was thinking. He decided to change the subject.

"How many have you made?"

"172."

"Shit! Sorry. But seriously? 172? Is that total, like all the times you've been shooting baskets or just today."

"Just today. I made 106 of them in a row."

"Sh...shoot. Aren't your arms tired?"

"Yeah."

"How long did it take?" Dave looked at his watch. It was only 2:30pm. "And shouldn't you be in school?"

"I don't know, an hour or something. I'm home schooled. This is my gym glass. Dad says I need to get a scholarship and sports are the only way since I'm home schooled."

"Do you play on a team?"

"Of course." She looked at him like he was stupid.

He didn't know how the whole home schooling / sports team thing worked. His own daughter didn't play sports and went to a regular public school. "When are you going to stop?"

"When I miss again I guess."

Swish.

Her dog came trotting across the yard and stopped when it saw Dave. Dave was a little afraid of dogs. He liked them, but he was nervous around them. And they sensed it. Like his therapist, they wanted to know why he was so nervous. Unlike his therapist, they often bit him, or tried to. He had taken a course once to become a dog trainer to get rid of whatever was in the way of getting along with dogs. He learned all the philosophy and commands and passed the written tests, but the instructor said he couldn't recommend him for a job because dogs didn't like him. Dave didn't even want a job – he had a job – but it still hurt. The guy was a real asshole. Dave wondered why people who love animals sometimes forget to be kind to people.

"Does your dog bite?" he asked the girl.

"No," she shook her head and put the ball down and ran over to the shaggy brown thing. "See?" she said and nuzzled the dog who accepted the hug but never took his eyes off Dave.

Children are so confused about love, Dave thought. They think giving and receiving it are the same. They think the things and people they love should behave the way they want them to. Love doesn't equal control Dave thought as he looked away from the dog.

"If you're scared of him, I can tie him up," the girl offered.

"No, don't do that. I'm fine."

"Do you want to take a shot?"

Dave stood up. "Sure, why not. I'm not very good, though."

"It's okay. Just bend your knees and keep your eye on the basket."

His own father had given him the same advice over and over. But it hadn't worked then and Dave doubted it would work now. He took the balk and bounced it a few times. He lifted it above his head, bent his knees, looked at the basket and launched the ball.

"Who the hell are you and why are you in my yard?"

Dave's shot bounced off the backboard and into the net.

"Yes!" said the girl. "Mom, it's okay, he's from the carpet place."

"Did you not give him my note?"

"I did, but he said he needed other stuff, so we waited for you to come back."

Dave wasn't exactly sure that was what they were doing, but the girl's explanation sounded good.

"You have no business in a yard with a little girl. Are you a pervert?"

"What? No, what she said..."

"Get out. I'm not buying carpet from your store anymore. I'm cancelling my order."

"Mom, he..."

"Quiet." She admonished her daughter before turning to Dave. "Look, leave now, and I won't call the police. You're a pervert watching my daughter jump around."

Dave's words were all jammed up together in his throat so he couldn't get any of them out. You are the shrew who left her alone, he would have said. You are the one who should be in trouble with the police. Unless eleven or twelve was old enough to be left alone. He didn't know. Then the dog came around the corner growling, so Dave backed away with his hands up, leaving everything unsaid.

"Buddy, come here," the girl called. "Sorry. That was a nice shot, mister!"

Dave turned around and put his hands in his pockets and started walking away. He walked past his car. He didn't feel like getting in. He just wanted to walk. He started to cry, angry tears and sad tears. He had been having fun, doing the right thing, he thought. Shit. He felt stupid and embarrassed crying, so he tried to think about something else. Something fun. But he couldn't for the life of him think of anything fun. He couldn't even come up with a picture of something fun, not even a picture of his elevator.

He walked a long time. He walked until he was lost, even though he had lived in this city since he was a teenager. He looked around for a street name, a landmark, the sun. Anything that would tell him where he was. Nothing helped. He stopped at the next intersection and thought about calling someone. But he'd left his phone in the car. He felt like a foreigner in the wrong train station. He saw a bus sign to the left and headed towards it, figuring he would take the bus somewhere. As he sat in the little plexiglass shelter trying to decipher the schedule, he heard the sounds of a basketball game behind him. The schedule showed no bus for an hour, so he decided to go see what was going on.

The court hardly merited the name. It was a patch of cracked asphalt surrounded partly by broken chain link fencing. The hoops had no nets. The men playing looked older, but they were all sinew and muscle. He had never seen a real basketball game except on television. It was noisier than he would have expected. He kept walking around all four sides of the court until he found a tree to lean against and watch. It was like watching musical theatre, he thought. The grunts and calls and body shots had to be choreographed. Everyone was so fast. It was beautiful. A shot didn't go in, and a player got the rebound and threw it back up before his feet even hit the floor. That one went in and the shooter did a handstand to celebrate. Such strength.

A tall guy in a headband on the other team picked up the ball and hurled it down the court. The shooter got back on defense so fast he was able to slap it out of its arc. The slap redirected the ball over the fence, and then they saw him.

"Hey sir, can you get that for us?" one of the players yelled at him.

"Uh, sure," Dave said and looked around for where the ball landed. He had taken his eye off the ball to watch the men watching it. The ball was wedged under the front bumper of an Audi. Dave pulled it free and jogged back to the fence and tried to throw it over. But something cramped in his back and the ball bounced off the fence and back to the Audi.

"Shit, man. You're useless," said the guy with the headband whose pass was tipped.

Dave was embarrassed and repeated his trip to the Audi.

"Don't be a jerk, Caesar You could have gotten it yourself. You okay?" the shooter called to Dave.

"I'm fine," Dave said. He limped with the ball toward the fence. The shooter had come out and took the ball from him.

"Thanks."

"No problem."

"Hey whitey, just keep on walking now okay? You've gotten your free show."

"Caesar, chill, what's the big deal? Nothing wrong with an audience. Or maybe he wants to play. You wanna play? Ramone needs a rest. He smokes, and he's got shit for wind." The guy talking threw the ball at the man who must be Ramone and laughed.

"I am still faster and better than you," Ramone said. "I smoke to level the playing field so I don't get bored with your sorry attempts to guard me."

Dave guessed he didn't really need to answer the question.

"Fine let him watch. Or maybe he wants to get us some Gatorade. You wanna get us some Gatorade, man? Huh? Think of it as the price of admission," Caesar said.

"Sure. Where should I go?" Dave was thirsty anyway and figured if he could find a market, he could ask someone how to get home. He was feeling a little dizzy, too.

"Caesar, seriously, don't be an asshole. Making some stranger get us drinks is mean."

"I don't mind." Dave could feel himself swaying.

"Hey, you all right, man? You look like shit," Ramone asked.

"I. . ." Dave crumpled to the ground.

"Shit!" Ramone sprinted to Dave and ripped open his shirt. He listened to his heart and breathing.

"Terrell, get my bag and my phone."

Terrell had been on the bench so he grabbed the bag and brought it to Ramone. Ramone grabbed his phone and called 911.

"I've got a heart attack victim here at the corner of Locust and River Road. Pulse is 110, he's gray, but he's conscious. I need an ambulance now."

"Terrell..."

"I'm going." And Terrell was off running toward the store. Not an EMT like Ramone, he still knew the white guy needed water or ice or something. Maybe Ramone was wrong, and it wasn't a heart attack. Maybe he was just hot. No way the cops wouldn't think they had done something to him. Rich white guy like that. They cannot let him die. He ran faster, as if Gatorade would save them all.

Casear and two of the other guys were tossing baskets and the rest were getting their things. Everyone saw enough accidents and death in this neighborhood that it wasn't interesting enough to hang around for. Plus Ramone was an EMT and he had this. He would tell them all what happened next week.

Terrell heard the ambulance in the distance. That was fast, he thought. He turned around and ran back to see Ramone getting into the ambulance with the guy, doing chest compressions and bleeding all over the guy.

"What the hell?"

"I cut my hand. I'm fine. Follow us."

"How did you do that?"

"The guy had a knife in his pocket."

"A knife?"

"A box cutter. It wasn't closed. It was an accident."

Terrell got on his bike and followed the ambulance, pedaling as fast as he could. The ambulance could run the lights, but it still had to slow down for them. He wasn't much

49

behind it when they got to the hospital. He knew why Ramone wanted him to follow them. The blood and the box cutter would make everyone suspicious.

The other EMT in the ambulance took Dave's phone out of the holder on his belt and called Abby. She was the first entry in his contacts list. She said she would meet them at the hospital. On the way there, Dave slid into unconsciousness. The emergency room doctors went into overdrive, and Ramone and Terrell were left to answer the admitting nurse's questions as best they could. Fifteen minutes later Abby burst in on a wave of panic and looked around for someone until she settled on Ramone and Terrell.

"Where is my husband?"

"Lady," Terrell started to say, but the admitting nurse interrupted him in a voice that was at once kind and curt.

"Ma'am, who is your husband, please?"

"David Adams. They called me. . ."

"He is in the operating room. You can wait here and the doctors will be out as soon as they know something. Coffee is down the hall, and we have a cafeteria on the second floor."

"Who are they, and why are they looking at me?"

The woman's anger and fear needed a target. Ramone had seen it before. but Terrell had not.

"Mrs. Adams, these men brought your husband in. Ramone is one of our EMTs."

She scanned them, taking in the blood on Ramone's shirt.

"Were you in a fight? What did you do to my husband? What did you do?"

"Look you fucking bitch, we helped him," Terrell said.

"Why was he in your neighborhood? How did you find him? What happened?"

"Our neighborhood? What the hell does that mean?"

"Security to the ER. Security to the ER."

"Ma'am, let me get you a chair over here," the nurse said and took Abby's arm.

"Terrell, we need to go," Ramone grabbed Terrell's arm to keep him from following and yelling at Abby some more, but he shook it off.

"She needs. . ."

"She needs nothing. She is upset. Let's go."

"But she got it all wrong. You should get the credit."

"It's okay. I love that you wish people were better, but they aren't. Wishing just makes you mad. And I don't need any credit." When he was sure no one was looking, Ramone kissed Terrell on the cheek. "Come on."

"Shit man. You're too nice to people."

Dave didn't wake up until the next day. When he did, he saw his ex-wife asleep on the chair. He felt like shit, but he was so happy to see her. Maybe their divorce was all a misunderstanding. Maybe they could get back together. He closed his eyes and tried to remember what happened. The last thing he remembered was the little girl.

"How many did she make?"

"Huh? What are you talking about?"

Before Dave could answer, his therapist swooped into the room. Nancy always swooped.

"What the fuck are you thinking having a heart attack at 44?"

"You told me not to curse."

"You're not cursing, I am."

He laughed out loud. "You're a great sister, but I am beginning to think you are a lousy therapist. Yesterday was the worst day ever. Your advice stinks."

"You get what you pay for. But you seem different, lighthearted. Maybe all those blockages in your arteries were making you depressed and angry at the world. This could be good." She turned to Dave's ex-wife, who was her usual silent self when the brother and sister got going.

"It's probably the meds," Dave said.

"Nope," Nancy said. "I think you'll be a new person after this." She turned around. "Hi Abby. How are you?"

"Fine, considering." Abby wasn't a big fan of Nancy's, but she couldn't put her finger on why.

Nancy knew things were always uncomfortable when the three of them got together, but it wasn't her problem now that Dave and Abby were divorced. It wasn't really her problem before, she added to herself.

"What are the doctors saying?" Nancy asked them both.

"Well, Dave has just woken up, so I doubt he knows much. All they have told me is that he had a severe heart attack, that they did quadruple bypass surgery, and that he'll need to spend some time in cardiac rehab and make radical changes in his diet if he wants to see Rachel grow up."

"Sounds like stuff doctors would say to anyone who had a heart attack."

"His was a textbook case they said."

"Well, it's nice to smack in the middle of the bell curve in something," Dave said. "Since you seem to have all the answers, Abby, how long will I have to be in the hospital?"

"They said it depends on the kind of support you have at home."

The two women looked at each other.

"I guess I'll be here for a while." The concept of a long recovery was unpleasant plus talking made him feel like shit, so he closed his eyes.

"No, we'll figure something out," said Abby. "The longer you're in the hospital, the more chance you have to pick up an infection."

"Good point," Nancy said, and studied him for a moment. "You look tired. We should go."

Dave didn't know how much time had passed since they left, but it was dark when the nurse came back in to give him his medicine. He drifted off to sleep.

The next day, his boss came to visit.

"How are you feeling, Dave?"

"Better than I probably should be, I guess, considering." Dave was pleased his boss remembered his new nickname.

"I talked to Abby last night and she filled me in. Take as much time as you need to heal. Your job will be there for you."

"That's a relief."

"But can I ask you a question if you feel up to it?"

"Sure."

"What happened at the Channing house?"

Dave pushed himself up on his right elbow so he could face his boss at least as a partial equal.

"What did Mrs. Channing say?"

"She just cancelled her order. She wouldn't say why. It wasn't a big order, I was just curious if, I don't know if the stress had anything to do with your heart attack."

"No workers' compensation claim from me, if that is what you're asking."

"No, well, yes to be honest, but I'm more worried about you," Sid said.

It was a lie, but one that made them both feel better, even though Dave also knew it was a lie.

"When I got there, her kid was shooing baskets in the backyard. Nobody else was home. So I talked to the kid and waited. I was actually a little worried that she was left alone. I thought about calling social services."

"Well, I am glad you didn't. That is the last thing we should be doing."

"Seriously? Why?"

"It would be bad for business. No one wants people in their homes who judge them."

"I never got in their home. When Mrs. Channing did come home, she wouldn't let me in. She accused me of being a pervert hanging out with her kid, so I left. It didn't stress me out."

That was not the whole truth, but this conversation wasn't about the truth.

"Okay, well, I am sorry you had to go through that. We all have those customers occasionally, right?"

"Yeah." Dave realized that there were really very few customers who were that unpleasant. The decency of most people when you were in their homes was the most surprising part. They may be jerks in the store, but on their own turf they were often much nicer, at least by the end of his visit.

"Well, I've got to run. Call me if you need anything. We'll see you when you're back to 100 percent, okay?"

"Sure. Thanks, Sid."

Dave breezed through his recovery and cardiac rehab. Abby and Nancy took turns spending a week at his house until they were sure he had the energy to care for himself. Now he was back on his own. He thought that would be rough, but he was wrong. He had never felt better in his life than he did one month after that wonderful heart attack. He felt like superman. He still didn't like ladders, though, so he hired someone to set up the basketball hoop he had delivered as a present to himself.

It was installed when he got home from his first solo trip to the grocery store. Nancy and Abby had been so good to him that he hadn't had to shop for, much less prepare, any of his meals. They went on with the royal treatment far longer than necessary. But he wasn't complaining, although he liked picking out his own food. He was going to try and be healthy, but he needed the occasional treat which neither woman allowed him.

The hoop looked good on his garage. Or goal, the salesman called it a goal.

Nancy drove up as he was gazing at it.

"So now you have hoop dreams? I would have thought you wouldn't want to have anything to do with basketball after your heart attack."

"Why? It saved my life."

"How? I thought watching that girl shoot baskets was what got you in trouble and led to your heart attack."

"And a man playing basketball saved me. I liked the girl though. There was something lucky about her. I was clearly going to have a heart attack anyway. What if I had had it while I was driving? Or on a plane? No, basketball saved my life, and I am going to learn how to play."

"Okay. Fine. Get the ball and I'll play with you."

"I'd rather shoot on my own for a while, try and get my shot down before I unleash my moves on you."

They both laughed.

"Plus, I have groceries to put away."

"Fine. My shoes are crap for running around anyway. Do you want to start coming back to the office?"

"I think I'd like to take a break from therapy. A longer break," he corrected himself. He hadn't seen Nancy in her official capacity since his heart attack.

"Okay, fine." He couldn't tell if she was hurt. "Do you want to go out to dinner this weekend?"

"Probably. Can I call you though? I'm going to try and have Rachel over for a visit."

"Wow. Are you up for that?"

"I think so. I feel really great."

"All right, I'm out then. Love you," Nancy swept back into her car, somehow managing to corral her scarves and skirt and jacket and bracelets into the cabin in one motion.

"Love you too," Dave said and waved as the green Subaru drove away. He wasn't the kind of guy to lust after cars, but Nancy's shiny, earnest and athletic looking car triggered a desire to go shopping. He took his groceries inside and turned on the computer to look at cars.

Quickly dissatisfied with what was in his price range, Dave decided to get up and call Abby to see if Rachel could come for the weekend. He was relieved to be able to leave a message. That would give Abby time to adjust to the idea. Rachel was eleven going on thirty her mother liked to say. Dave didn't see the thirty part – she just seem like a kid. Sometimes she reminded him of himself at that age, and other times she seemed so much cooler. She had just quit gymnastics and was starting to put on weight. Dave's hope was that she would like playing ball with him and then go out for the team and lose the weight and they would have this great father daughter bond as a result. It could happen, he told himself, if he did everything right. If Abby would let him have her for Friday night as well, he would buy tickets for the UNC women's game.

He grabbed his new ball and headed outside to inaugurate his hoop. Goal. He didn't know what to call it. But dribbling was harder than it looked. His ball smacking the ground sounded nothing like the gentle, rhythmic drumming the Channing girl gave the ball before she shot and less than nothing like Ramone's rapid and powerful dribbling. He remembered that when he watched the men playing, it seemed like the ball sprung back from the court faster than the player threw it down. Dave didn't know enough about physics to know if that were possible. It will take time he told himself. He picked up the ball, took a deep breath and shot the ball as best he remembered in the direction of the basket. It was high enough but far right. He repeated his effort several times and got no closer to the basket. Frustrated, he sat down. Maybe I just need to get used to holding it, develop a feel for the ball. I'll just carry it around with me like the kids do, he thought.

The phone rang, and he scrambled inside to get it, hoping it was Abby.

"Hello?"

"She's not keen about it, but I told her how important this weekend is for you, so she's willing to go."

His own daughter is willing to spend time with him? Is that the best he can hope for?

"Um, okay. Do you think I should. . ." Should what? Dave couldn't complete his own thought. Wasn't he doing enough differently already?

"No, no. She's just getting to that age. You guys will have fun, I'm sure. I know I'm glad to get her out of the house. For her sake. I mean, she needs a change. She needs a father."

"I'd like to be one again."

"So I'll drop her off after school on Friday?"

"Sure. I'll take a half day so I'll be home."

"Okay bye."

"Bye."

Dave wished Rachel was excited about the weekend, but at least he would have her. She'll enjoy it, he thought. She has to.

Dave did take the ball to work the next day. He took a gym bag too, so it looked like he was going to work out. Everyone had been really nice to him since his heart attack, but he knew he would have to start making sales again to really be a part of the team.

His office phone buzzed.

"Hi Sally," he answered.

"Hi Dave. I've got a couple here to see you. Said they were in a couple of months ago and you helped them?"

"Sure, I'll be right out."

Excellent, he thought. This sale is in the bag. He straightened his tie and checked his teeth in the mirror he kept in his desk drawer. All good.

Walking to the front of the store, he didn't recognize the couple standing there. He would need to get better at that, at remembering names and faces.

"Hi, I'm Dave. It's good to see you both again."

"Thanks for remembering us," the man stuck out his hand.

Was it really this easy?

"Well, of course. But I don't remember your project. . ."

"Basement re-do," the woman said, and Dave's new heart sank. This would be cheap carpet. No one wants wool for the basement.

"Right, right. Have you narrowed it down?"

"Well, we want something blue."

The three of them spent the next hour wandering the showroom, looking at options. They were stuck between two choices, one a lot more expensive, when Dave suggested they get a soda in his office. The man – Dave still hadn't asked them to repeat their names – noticed the basketball.

"You play ball in college?"

It was easier to go along, sort of. "That was a long time ago." He'd heard his boss use the phrase.

"Ain't that the truth," the man said and patted his gut. Dave had gotten soft over the years, but didn't have a gut like this guy's. That was a fact he was very proud of.

"What position?"

"Forward," Dave said in a panic, remembering his height and hoping there would be no more questions.

"Could I get that soda?" the wife asked.

"Of course. I'm so sorry." Relieved, Dave pulled three Cokes from the mini-fridge. "No need to talk about sports when there are big decisions to be made."

"That's the perfect time to talk about sports, the man said, grabbing Dave's ball."

"Oh, this is nice and new. You're still breaking it in."

"Yup," was all Dave had to offer. Eventually, they decided on the cheaper carpet, but Dave sold them on a decent pad. That was where the real mark-up was. He was starving when they left, but he felt good. He decided to call it a day.

That night he had some luck at the goal. He made a few baskets and managed to dribble and trot at the same time. He worked up a good sweat, even though he took frequent breaks as his doctor told him to. Feeling that a hole in his life had been plugged, he went inside to shower and make some whole wheat pasta with broccoli and chicken. It wasn't too bad, just bland.

Finally it was Friday, the day everything was going to change. He left work at noon with his boss' blessing. One decent sale and he was back in the club. He checked his watch, grabbed his ball and bag, and decided to meet Rachel at school. He left Abby a message, explaining the new plan.

The school looked so different to Dave, but he couldn't put his finger on why. He parked in a visitor's spot, and headed to the main office to get a pass. He had decided on the way over to talk to the basketball coach and see if there was room for Rachel on the team. Hell, maybe he could even shot a few baskets with him.

When Dave got to the gym, a man in polyester shorts with a whistle was putting five girls through some drills.

"Can I help you?" The coach called out to him. The tone in his voice was more aggressive than Dave had hoped. Dave hadn't even realized the dribbling had stopped.

"Um, I'm Dave Adams. My daughter Rachel is a student here, and she'd like to start playing basketball."

"Really? Okay. Um girls, ten lay-ups each. I'll be right back." He jogged over to Dave and stopped to shake his hand.

"I'm Skip Tanner."

"Dave Adams."

"Got that the first time, sir. Come on in my office and we can talk."

"Sure," Dave said, following the coach's quick stride. He wanted to watch the girls a little longer, but knew that would get him the pervert label pretty fast. Skip didn't seem like he was going to be easy to talk to, but Dave wasn't giving up hope.

Skip closed the glass door behind them and motioned Dave into a seat. Skip sat on the edge of his desk, making himself taller than Dave.

"So, you want your daughter to play basketball? Follow in your footsteps?" The smile was the most insincere Dave had ever seen. He felt like he was walking into a trap. There would be no friendly game of one on one with this man.

"Yes," he said, answering the first question only. He was getting good at ambiguity.

"Well, you know it's the middle of the season. Is she good?"

"I don't know."

"She's never played?"

"No, but I know she wants to."

"Why isn't *she* talking to me?"

"She will. I just had some time to kill before picking her up, and I thought I'd meet you."

"Okay, fair enough," Skip said, obviously meaning the opposite. "But she has to try out, and since it's the middle of the season, she's going to have to have some mad skills to make the team. Even the bench. We have a lot of good girls who have been here all season."

He was completely screwing up, Dave realized. Yeah, this guy was a jerk, but Dave was a fool. Of course Rachel would have to wait until next season. Shit.

"Never mind, I don't know what I was thinking. We'll come back in the fall, before the next season."

"Good idea, I think she'll like it better. You know, to start with the rest of the girls. I can give you some information on summer camps to work on her skills. I run one here she may like. It never hurts to impress the coach, right?" Skip opened his file drawer and handed Dave a stack of brochures. "Mine is the red one."

"Okay, thanks. Thanks for your time."

They shook hands again, and Skip held the door for him, making Dave duck under his arm and get a whiff of his armpit.

Skip returned to the court as if nothing had happened. "Okay, girls, lets do some box sprints. On my mark...."

Dave pulled open the heavy doors to the gym into the peace and quiet of the hall. He went back to his car, visitor pass still on, and waited for Rachel there. When he saw her, she looked so little and sloppy compared to the girls in the gym. But she's so young, he told himself, she has time to get good. Maybe not next year, but by the time she gets to juniors, she'll be a good player. I need to be patient, he told himself.

He got out of the car and waved. She saw him and stuck her hand up almost imperceptibly and headed for his car.

"Hi sweetie."

"Hi Dad."

"Are you ready for the weekend?"

"I guess. I have to get my bag from Mom – it's in her car."

"I called and asked her to drop it at my house."

"Okay."

"What do you want to do before the game?"

"I'm hungry."

"Okay, let's eat. Where?"

"Wherever."

It was starting to rain.

"How about pizza?" Dave asked, turning the key in the ignition and pulling out, nearly hitting another car.

"Okay."

They had pizza in a loud sports bar next to the campus. They left the game at halftime. Rachel was bored.

"Dad?" Rachel asked on the way home.

"Yeah?"

"Can you take me back to Mom's tonight? I just feel weird."

"Weird like sick, or weird like you don't want to sleep at my house?"

"Both, Dad."

Dave tried to take some deep breaths. He didn't know if he wanted to yell or cry.

"Okay, sweetie. Okay. Sure. Okay."

At his house, Rachel got her bag and Dave called his wife to let her know of the change of plans.

"Oh crap, I'm sorry," Abby said.

"It's okay. We can try again. I was rushing her. Maybe we need a few more outings before she spends the night."

"You are being a prince, Dave. She'll see it. It's just a bad age. I'll be right over."

Dave thought back to the girls at the school gym. "Maybe." Or maybe it's me.

After Abby and Rachel left, Dave got a beer – he was allowed one a day according to his new heart healthy diet – and his basketball and went out to shoot. He heard his phone ringing but ignored it. He finished his beer and had to pee, but he didn't want to go inside. He hid himself in the rhododendron and solved his problem. He was zipping up as headlights pulled into his driveway, and he was bouncing the ball when Nancy got out.

"You okay? Abby called me and said you sounded funny on the phone."

"Really? But I'm fine." He aimed the ball at the basket and bent his knees and pushed it into its arc.

It hit the side of the house. Not even the backboard, the side of the house.

"That's 106."

"106 what?"

"106 baskets in a row."

"Seriously?"

"Yup. I'm going for a record."

Dave bounced the ball twice, looked up, and shot the ball. It hit the side of the house.

"107. You can count for me now that you are here, so I can focus on shooting. Okay?"

Nancy caught herself before she said what was in her mind.

"Okay," she said instead.

WHERE BIRDS GO IN A HURRICANE

Tucker stopped suddenly and threw himself body and soul into sniffing the mulch around the base of the neighbor's camellia bush. Susan used to get frustrated at the dog's frequent and prolonged stops, thinking Tucker was wasting his valuable exercise time. Then she read somewhere that inhaling and sorting through all of the diverse odors in the world engaged a dog's mind which was as important to its well being as physical exercise. So she taught herself to stand still and let Tucker do whatever he wanted with his time. Sometimes Tucker sniffed without marking, sometimes the marking was an afterthought, as if he remembered he really had to pee, and sometimes it was instantaneous. Susan wondered what specific smell triggered his need to pee on a particular spot. But it didn't matter, she told herself, we're out for a walk for Tucker's sake not mine.

So she used Tucker's many, many stops to plan her day or just look around and breathe. She would try and exhale for twice as long as she inhaled. Five counts in, ten counts out. It made her feel like she was accomplishing something. Today while exhaling at the camellia Susan saw something she often did: a crow being chased by half a dozen smaller birds. The smaller birds looked like robins, but they were moving so fast it was hard to tell. Susan kept watching the aerial dogfight and noticed that the crow had something in its beak. A twig or some other piece of nesting material, Susan figured. The things animals fight over, she thought, as if there aren't a thousand twigs on the ground that would be just as good. On its second pass, the crow dropped one of the twigs, and even from half a block away Susan could see that the twig was a baby bird. As soon as it hit the pavement, one of the robins went to it, quickly decided there was nothing he or she could do, and flew off to resume the chase. The crow had another baby still in its mouth that needed saving. Why had the greedy crow taken two? Susan could see the one on the pavement struggling, trying to lift a featherless wing, its beak opening and closing, letting out faint cries that Susan hoped she was imagining. She knew she should put the baby bird out of its misery, but there was no way she could kill the poor thing.

Tucker pulled on his leash, oblivious to the bird tragedy and ready to move on, and that snapped her back to her life. She led him across the street to avoid the baby bird. Tucker was a good dog, never asking for more than the two walks a day Susan could make time for. She wasn't able to pay as much attention to him as before Kendall was born. But that was the way of the world for dogs in her neighborhood and probably in neighborhoods all over the world.

They completed the block, and when they got home, Greg was getting ready to leave for work. She couldn't bring herself to tell him about the bird, although the image of its struggle against death would not leave her mind. She wondered what happened to the other one.

"I gave Kendall her breakfast. I've got a conference call with the Hong Kong office, so I'll be late tonight." He bent down to rub Tucker's head and let the dog lick his cheek. Tucker loved the taste of Greg's shaving cream. Susan loved that Greg, who kept his hair short, his eyebrows trimmed and his clothes pressed, and was otherwise careful about the way he presented himself to the world, was so tolerant of dog spit on his face.

"Okay. I'll just make sandwiches for dinner."

"Perfect. Bye to my beautiful girls." He kissed Kendall on the top of her head and Susan full on the lips.

It was a better kiss than any of her friends got from their husbands, but he was still out the door before Susan could say goodbye. Greg always moved in a higher gear than she did in the mornings, but Susan was feeling more sluggish than usual today. She forced herself to start cleaning up the breakfast dishes. School would be out for the summer soon, and she needed to start making arrangements for camps and activities to fill the void.

"Mommy?"

"Yes, sweetie?"

"What happens to the animals when the weather is bad?"

"Baby, why are you worried about that? It's a nice day outside."

"Not on the television."

Susan looked to the mini box mounted under the kitchen cabinets and sure enough the news was showing hurricane footage from Florida.

"Oh. Well, you know we bring Tucker in when it rains, and other people take care of their pets too." Kendall was too young to need to know about all the ways people could neglect or be cruel to what they were supposed to protect. She was okay with lying to her child for now. She would worry about when the right time was to introduce Kendall to life's harsher lessons when she was a little older.

"What about wild animals?"

"Wild animals are smart, honey. They know what to do in all kinds of weather."

"What about birds? Where do they go in a hurricane?"

Susan stopped loading the dishwasher. The question was so strange and beautiful it tore a piece of her heart right out of her chest. That was what parenting often felt like to Susan. Having pieces torn out of her, replaced by something else. Usually the something else was a piece of Kendall that she discarded to make room for something new, like a snake shedding its skin. Being a mother felt like a slow process of being replaced by your child, and Susan liked it.

She turned and looked at her daughter who was sitting at the breakfast table. Such a stupid name for a piece of furniture, Susan thought for the umpteenth time, as if you couldn't eat lunch of dinner there.

"So where do they go, Mommy?" Kendall's blue eyes stared into hers and waited patiently. Her daughter was so exquisitely beautiful it took Susan's breath away every time she looked squarely at her, which she tried not to do very often because it felt like a drug addiction. Kendall was about to turn seven, and Susan wondered if she would ever stop having that reaction.

"I don't know sweetie. I guess some of them are blown around, but maybe some of them can hide. Like when we see birds fly under the eaves of houses."

"But what if the houses are blown away?"

"The birds can fly away before anything happens. And hurricanes don't last very long."

"But longer than earthquakes, right?"

"Yes, baby, longer than earthquakes. But not too long."

Satisfied, Kendall went back to work on her drawing.

She had a twin who died in childbirth. They were going to name him Van, after Van Morrison who at the time was still Susan's favorite singer. Now, she couldn't listen to him without remembering. When the baby was stillborn, the name felt so inappropriate. What name would be appropriate for a dead baby Greg had asked her, angry and wild eyed and desperate with grief. They needed to fill out the hospital paperwork, so Van it was. Susan wanted to save the name for a live baby, in case they ever had another one. She had always thought she would have two or three children. But Greg wanted a vasectomy and talked Susan into it. He said he couldn't deal with the fear something would happen again after nine months of anticipation and hope. Susan didn't feel she had the right to ask him to try.

Van had only one arm and no eyes. They took one picture of him, a Polaroid, but Susan threw it away immediately. She would never forget him anyway, and she preferred to imagine him as she did when he was in her womb, perfect and beautiful. One of the nurses suggested she keep a journal of her feelings that she could one day show to Kendall when she was old enough to know about her brother. Susan wrote religiously for the first several months. But then Kendall started sleeping less and needing more of her time, so the writing fell away.

Something about the dropped baby bird made her want to find a notebook.

"I'll be right back sweetie. Are you okay for a minute?"

"Yeah, Mommy. I'm fine."

Kendall could draw for hours. It was one of the things Susan loved most about her. She was astonished at the way Kendall could lose herself in the worlds she drew. And they weren't pretty scenes, usually buildings and monsters, but they made her happy.

Susan went upstairs and into her husband's office to hunt for a legal pad. He bought them by the case, in yellow. She hated his office and almost never went in. It was decorated in burgundy and blue, like a hotel. The colors made her gag. But Greg had pretty good taste in everything else. It was as if he had some primordial need for an ugly office. She felt it came from the same part of him that needed a perfect lawn. She didn't mind weeds and preferred light, neutral colors, but she knew she had to compromise and these two things were small enough in the big picture. Her friends fought over every decorating detail in their houses. Susan saw what it did to their husbands.

All the pads on Greg's desk had writing on them, so she started opening drawers to look for an unused one. It never occurred to her to worry about what she would find.

She found the legal pads, a big stack of them. When she reached in to take the top one, she saw that behind the stack was a fat envelope wrapped in a rubber band that was mashed in the right way to look like it held photos. She smiled, and slid off the rubber band, excited to see which of their photos Greg kept close to his work. But they were all photos of him with a little boy who had no eyes and one arm.

Susan screamed. Tucker barked, and his nails scrabbled for purchase on the kitchen floor as he raced to her.

"Mommy," Kendall called out. "Are you okay?" Her little feet thumped when she slid off her chair and hit the ground.

Susan felt she heard all of this from the bottom of a pit. Tucker appeared at the doorway of Greg's office and growled, in case whatever made Susan scream was something that needed to be scared away.

"It's okay, Tucker," Susan managed to whisper. Tucker wagged his tail and came and sat next to her chair, leaning his narrow, furry body into hers in the only way dogs can hug.

"Did you get a boo - boo, Mommy?" Kendall asked when she appeared.

"No, baby, I was just startled." Susan had to pull herself together. Kendall didn't have much use for a mommy in a pit. "It's almost time to go to school. Are you ready?"

"In two seconds." Kendall picked that phrase up from Greg, and it always made Susan smile. "I've got to finish my drawing."

"Okay, well hurry."

Kendall marched quickly back to the kitchen, swinging her arms like a cartoon soldier the way she always did when Susan told her to hurry.

Her leaving threw Susan back into the pit. Tucker came over and nudged Susan's hand. He knew it wasn't okay, but he didn't know what to do. There was nothing to bite or bark at.

Susan and Tucker sat there for a while, until Susan's mind understood that the child in the photo was not Van. It couldn't be Van. Van was dead. The child in the photo looked about ten or eleven. Even if Van had lived, he would be Kendall's age, seven. Her reality stitched itself back together in fits and starts.

Susan dragged herself upright. "Come on, Tucker, you've got to go in your crate. Thanks for coming to my rescue." Tucker wagged his tail.

She decided to go to see Greg at work. This couldn't wait. She didn't trust herself to sit with this knowledge and her questions and not lose her mind. Why did he have these pictures? Susan took one of the photos and put it in her pocket and fished a cookie for the dog out of the jar on Greg's desk. The boy is not Van; Susan had a hold of that fact. But is he Greg's son? A strange mixture of nausea and hope flooded through Susan.

Kendall trotted happily to the car, thankfully oblivious to what the dog could sense. When they got to school, Susan hugged her and kissed her nose, their usual farewell. She watched as Kendall ran to the school, backpack flopping with each step. Two other little girls joined her even before she got halfway across the lawn.

To delay the confrontation Susan stopped for coffee once she got to Greg's building. The building had a lovely café on the ground floor. She didn't need the caffeine; her heart was beating erratically enough. So decaf it was, even though it always tasted flat to her. She poured cream and sugar in the coffee which helped a little. She tried to read a newspaper someone had left on one of the tables, but all she could do was look at the pictures. Pictures of war and golf and celebrities were what the news boiled down to today. She went to the bathroom to make sure she didn't look like a crazy woman.

She was nervous and thought about abandoning her plan – maybe she could make everything okay by just forgetting what she saw. But when the elevator doors opened at the 14th floor, she got out.

"Oh, Susan, how nice to see you. I'll ring Greg."

"Greg, Susan's here." A pause. "Okay." She put the phone down. "Go on back."

"Thanks. How's your elbow?" Susan tried to sound normal. Joanne and Susan were occasional tennis partners.

"Getting better. Maybe next week we can have a short match?"

"Sounds great. I'll call you," Susan said, knowing she was lying.

When Susan walked around the corner, Greg was putting a file away.

"Hi honey, what brings you here? Is Kendall okay?" Greg got up and walked around the desk to kiss her, concern furrowing his brow.

Susan pulled the photo out of her pocket, and handed it to him. He looked at it for what seemed like forever. Susan sat down and waited for the accusations. "Where did you get this, why were you going through my desk." But she knew they wouldn't come. It would have helped to fight, she thought, although she didn't know what it would help.

"Susan, meet Xavier."

Greg handed the photo back to her and sat down in his chair. He closed his eyes for a long time and then opened them and looked at her, clearly waiting.

"Who is he? Is he your son?"

"No, he is not my son. But he is very special to me. I, I was so lost. You had Kendall to care for, but in my dreams, Van kept floating in my dreams. I asked doctors and searched for someone with his same. . . handicap." Greg told his story as if he had been waiting for the opportunity.

"Do you want to leave us?" Susan fully expected his answer to be no. She was just being noble.

"Yes. No." Greg closed his eyes as if it were easier to speak if he didn't look at Susan. "Yes. I think so." He opened his eyes.

Susan looked at Greg. He looked like a stranger, like someone she would walk by on the street and not notice. All those kisses, those kisses that made her feel superior and safe, they were fake, Susan thought, feeling suddenly off balance. She reached for the only handle there was anymore.

"Where does he live? I need to meet him."

"Let me call his mother and see if we can come by for a visit. Joanne?" He shouted his secretary's name instead of using the intercom. She hurried in. Greg didn't ever shout.

"Yes?"

"Cancel anything I have for the rest of today, and tomorrow, please."

Joanne looked at Greg, then at Susan. "Of course."

She closed the door when she left.

Greg pulled out a disposable cell phone, not the iPhone he usually used. So that was how he kept everything secret. He pressed two keys.

"Maria? It's Greg. Can we come for a visit? Susan found the photos of Xavier and I think she needs to meet him."

Susan could hear Maria's voice, but couldn't make out the words.

"We knew this might happen."

She realized Maria was speaking Spanish. She didn't know Greg understood Spanish. Apparently, she didn't know much anymore and she was suddenly scared.

"No, I don't think she'll make a scene." Greg looked up at Susan.

More Spanish came through the phone.

"Okay. Thanks. We'll be there in an hour."

They took Susan's car, but Greg drove. There wasn't much traffic on the streets in the middle of the morning and they were soon on the highway heading east. The harder Susan tried to figure out what she thought, what she wanted to do and say, the more a blackness filled her mind. She was so consumed with both jealousy and sympathy for this other mother that the emotions cancelled each other out and left her numb. She couldn't feel anything for Greg. Greg drove without looking at her, as if he knew.

"Stop the car," she said when she saw an exit sign coming up. "I don't want to go anymore."

Greg took that next exit off the highway and pulled into a gas station.

"Are you sure?" he asked after he turned the car off.

"Yes. For now. I don't know about later."

"Okay."

He started the car.

"So would you love Kendall more if she were disfigured? I could make that happen, you know. I could go crazy and throw acid on her, back the car over her. You know, something like that." Susan stared at the side of Greg's head. "Just because she is beautiful doesn't mean she doesn't need you."

"I know that. I just need. . ."

"You need to be the fucking hero." The anger burst through her sadness and confusion, like a superhero arriving on the scene to rescue a train full of people. "You have held it against me that I moved on. I see that now. What did you want me to do, fall apart? Leave Kendall with no functioning parents? It's not her fault she lived and is beautiful."

"I don't want you to do anything, other than let me live the life I want."

"And that life doesn't include us?"

"Maybe not. This is a bit of a shock for me, too."

"So I need to feel sorry for you? You didn't think I would find out about your secret life?"

"I thought I would tell you one day. I just hadn't figured out when. I don't see Xavier that often, maybe once a week."

"Do you send them money?"

"Yes, but not much. We have plenty. We don't miss it."

"Kendall will miss you."

"That's bullshit, and you know it. She'll have you and you make a perfect little pair."

"What's that supposed to mean?"

"You both roll through life, making friends, making cookies, making plans. As if nothing bad is ever going to happen."

"He was my child too, you bastard."

"I saw how horrified you were when you looked at his body."

"So? He was horrible looking. He was broken and dead. He was scary looking. He wasn't a person. It doesn't mean I didn't love the idea of him and don't miss him. I loved him the whole time he was in my body. We never talk about him anymore. Now I know why. You replaced him."

"And you didn't. You run as far as you can from anything ugly in life. And Kendall will too. I don't want to be around people like you."

So he thought what she did to keep the house running and their daughter fed and dressed and cared for was all she was. Then Susan realized that was all she showed him. How could he know what else was there?

"You really think there is something morally superior about loving a deformed person than a beautiful person?"

"Yes."

"I can't believe you don't see it's just not that simple," Susan said. "Do you love Xavier only for the way he looks?"

"I only know that I need to be there for him. We have it so easy..."

"You think love is easier for beautiful people? You think life is? You are one stupid, mean son of a bitch." Getting angrier felt good, less confusing, less like dying.

"Well, it certainly isn't easier for the freaks and forgotten."

"The point is," Susan said, "is that it's not easy for anyone. No one should be using a yardstick to measure pain that they know nothing about."

"I think the point is to try and do what you can to create some balance in the world. And you seem to only care about your own little piece of the world."

"So you're atoning for our so-called easy life by playing part time daddy to Xavier. And what, part-time husband to his mother?"

"I only give her money and see Xavier. We are not lovers."

Susan didn't know if she cared. She could feel that the bond between them was already broken. The thought of him ever touching her again made her feel sick.

"How could you keep such a secret for so long?"

"I don't know," Greg said. "It was hard at first, but then it got easier."

He waited for her to say something and when she didn't after several minutes, he put the car in gear and drove back to his office.

Susan was numb on the drive back, but when they got to Greg's office, she got angry again.

"You actually think you deserve the luxury of choosing who to love?"

"Of course. We all do. At one time, I chose you, you chose me," Greg said.

"We didn't choose Kendall. She showed up. She is alive. She is in our house. I have to love her. You have to love her. She deserves that. There is no choice any more once a living thing depends on you. You can't chase your fantasy of some other kind of heroic, martyred love. You love who is in front of you."

Of course, Susan realized as soon as she said it, people do it every day. People stop loving who they are supposed to love.

"The beauty of love is in the loving. Not the receiving. If I could, I would. But I don't look at Kendall and feel love. I feel a kind of revulsion. And that can't be good for her either. I can't change how I feel."

"Yes, you can."

"I don't want her in my life. She is too perfect."

Susan couldn't believe what she was hearing. "How is that bad?"

Greg didn't say anything.

"Do you love Xavier?"

"Sometimes I am so consumed with love for him I feel physical pain. And that feels good." He paused as if he had to absorb what he said. "I'm sorry I hurt you." Then he got out and slid into the revolving doors.

Susan didn't ask if he was coming home. She didn't know if she wanted him to. She felt like one of Kendall's birds, looking for a place to ride out the hurricane. It was right around noon, and the sidewalks were starting to fill up. She had three hours before she had to pick Kendall up. She moved into the driver's seat and did a u-turn to get back on the highway heading west.

She stopped at her favorite beach and parked the car. She sat in the car and felt the sadness creep over her and into her every pore. Her skin felt as heavy as lead and she didn't know if she could carry it around. The wind was whipping and she could see three kite surfers in the distance. She took off her shoes and threw them in the back seat, opened the car door and carried her lead skin over the dunes and down to the beach.

The sign read: "The beach is closed. No swimming or surfing. A juvenile great white shark was spotted close to shore on Tuesday."

It's not like Susan was going to get in the water anyway, but the information on the sign still startled her.

"That sign is bullshit," said a woman who just appeared at Susan's shoulder. "I mean, the ocean is never safe. So long as there aren't any seals around and you don't swim when the sun is low, you're as fine as you would be on the highway. More fine. It makes people think if there isn't a sign, it's safe. It just hacks me off. I mean how can that be safe, the ocean's teeming with life, and why should it be? Why do we always need things to be safe?"

The woman looked at Susan for agreement.

"You're right."

"Damn right I am. Sorry, I get riled up at the city. Plus, if I'm angry, I'm not as scared. Have a nice day." The woman pulled on her goggles and walked into the waves.

FALLOUT SHELTER

If I were taller, it might have worked. I knew the head and the heart were the only decent targets, but my arms just weren't long enough to point the barrel squarely at either one and still be able to reach the trigger. I thought about sawing off the barrel, but not for long. I'm not even sure we have a saw. I guess I could have tried harder to jury-rig a set up. My one effort was to sit on the floor and put my right big toe on the trigger, aiming and steadying the barrel with my knees and hands. It was a disaster. The barrel was pointing at my left shoulder. I tried to nudge it closer to my chest which made the gun slip out of my awkward embrace. As we toppled, it or I knocked the lamp and the trash can over and ripped off part of my toenail. Butch, our fat tabby cat, screeched and ran for her life from the noise.

I don't care what people say, suicide is not the easy way out. Even attempted suicide is damn hard. If it wasn't going to be easy, I wasn't going to do it. That realization made me laugh, since refusing to take the easy path is what got me here.

I put the gun down lengthways on the desk. It served nicely as a giant paperweight, even though it teetered a little. My desk was cluttered with files and papers that came home with me when I was fired last week. The mounded white pile looked like frosting, transforming my walnut desk into a chocolate cupcake. The bay window was open letting in a breeze that stirred the leaves of the ficus and would have made hay with the papers but for the gun. I pondered the photos along the back edge of my desk. They were the same as those that graced offices everywhere, except now in duplicate. Two photos of me and Mary, Mary and the kids, and each child separately.

"I'm sorry, Mary," I said, scanning all the images of her before settling on the driftwood framed photo of us on the beach in Maine. It was taken five years ago, I think. That was the last time we took a vacation together. Not for lack of money or time, but rather lack of desire. Neither of us seemed to want a break from the safe routine of life, until now. "But I did what I had to do."

Mary and I bought this gun soon after we moved into our first house a whole lifetime ago. The house was a rental that had seen better days, but we were lucky to get it. We had just gotten engaged. With a home and a yard, an almost-wife and a new puppy to protect, as well as my own manhood to define, the gun seemed an appropriate response to our sketchy neighborhood. Our bedroom was on the side facing the alley where strange, scrabbling noises often originated. Probably raccoons or opossums people said, but this was still the South, and I knew it wouldn't hurt to be prepared for the worst. The old house wasn't easy to secure; the windows were low to the ground and some didn't lock properly. We had an alarm system, but we couldn't afford to buy the equipment to arm each of the windows, and we couldn't set it at night because the puppy might set off the motion detector. Still, I loved that house. It came with great neighbors, the kind who were open-minded and threw lavish parties and shared flowers and vegetables from their gardens over the back fence. Mary and I didn't have one green thumb between us. The house sat on a hill. It was one story with a white painted brick exterior and a carport instead of a garage. It looked as if sometime in the mid 1950s, a Midwestern ranch house met and married a Louisiana shotgun house and produced 320 Beechnut Lane. (It was the perfect address since I studied trees at the time. Mary and I reveled in meaningful coincidences like that when we were young as proof of the perfection of our bond.) There was only one hallway, about two-thirds of the way to the back, sort of a square on the east side of the house. It separated the master bedroom from the other two bedrooms and from the kitchen. Other than that, the rooms opened directly into each other. You would think it would be weird, but it was perfect for us. The oddities made us feel special and clever, like our house was a tiny maze for which only we had the map. It would be horrible now. We have grown to need rooms that can more easily be closed off.

A policeman friend advised us that a shotgun was the best weapon for home defense, especially since neither Mary nor I knew how to shoot or wanted to learn. He explained that only the most determined or whacked out criminals would stick around once they heard the sound of a shell being loaded in the chamber. Kah-chek. That made sense to me, so one Saturday I went to a gun show in a convention center somewhere in one of our northern suburbs. It seemed best that Mary not go. I remember that I paid less than $200 cash for the gun and two boxes of ammunition. The gun is black and shiny and surprisingly heavy with what seems to be a fake wood handle, and it has a shorter barrel than those shotguns you see in westerns. But still not short enough for my purpose today. Maybe those really long guns in the movies were rifles anyway. I don't know.

We kept it close by in that first house, under the bed. When we moved a year later to a bigger house in a better neighborhood, it went into a box in a hall closet. It has lived in hall or basement closets in each house ever since. Recently Mary confessed that for years she would take the box and slide it under the bed whenever I went out of town on business. Maybe that's what made me think of it today. I've never shot it and neither has Mary, as far as I know. We were both tempted early on, just out of curiosity, but not so much as the years went by. Curiosity died along with a lot of other things.

I put the gun and its ammunition back into their box and onto the top shelf of the hall closet next to the study. The ammunition is probably bad anyway. Because Mary likes the gun hidden, it lives under the old beaver fur hat I got in Russia on a student trip decades ago and Mary's father's navy coat. Mary used to wear the coat when we were camping or working in the yard or when she was trying to look particularly bohemian during a phase she went through in the late 1980s. I loved her in it. I've never worn the hat; it doesn't get cold enough where we live. But I won't get rid of it even though a big hat like that on a man as slight as I am would probably look a little funny. Not only am I short, I'm thin. I don't take up much space.

Thirty years and three houses ago, she might have been on my side. Hell, ten years even. But things have changed. Now we spend our time apart even when we are in the same room. Somewhere along the way it went from occasionally not liking something the other person did to actually not liking the other person. Was it a piling up of little differences or a lightning bolt we managed not to notice? Was it more me than her, or her than me? I don't know. Not that the answer really matters, I guess. I would say I have changed by shedding the non-essential parts of me. The parts you pick up to function in a society you no longer believe in, the experimental parts and the parts you craft to please others. She, I guess, would say that those parts of me were essential to her. Mary likes civilization and its rules.

I wish we were still close enough to weather this storm. Change is as inevitable as death, and losing a job is not the worst thing, even though it did drive me to dig out the shotgun. I think it was more curiosity than a real death wish. I had time on my hands, and I was alone in the house. That must be how kids get in trouble. I don't want to die. I have sacrificed enough to be able to keep my life.

A few friends from work took me out to lunch last Friday, the day after I cleaned out my desk when emotions were still raw. Lunch was a nice gesture, but my friends were clearly uncomfortable. They were either ashamed they didn't support me or they suffered from the effort of hiding their opinion that what I did was stupid and wrong. We weren't really close friends anyway. It was a nice enough lunch, though, and the group paid for mine. We walked to the parking lot in a flurry of handshakes and back slaps and good lucks. Frank lingered and then asked me to come to his car with him. I wasn't sure what to expect.

"Shelly made you this," he said as he pulled a frozen, foil-wrapped dish from a cooler in the backseat of his old Honda. "It's a chicken lasagna."

I held out my hands to take the dish, which was quite heavy and still icy cold. "Frank, we're not destitute. I've got some savings and investments... ."

"I know, I know. And it's just what she does, whether you've had a baby or a death in the family or moved into the neighborhood. It's a disposable pan."

"Or got fired."

"Or lost your job." Frank looked down and shifted his weight. He is a mountain of a man with two bad knees. He could have worn my fur hat, I thought. "Maybe something will come up after things settle down."

"Maybe. Thank you Frank. Really. And tell Shelly thanks too. I'm sure Mary will appreciate a night or two off from cooking. We probably won't be going out much."

"You're welcome. Well, I'll see you later, right?" Frank said as he opened his door and lowered his bulk into the driver's seat.

"Sure."

Frank closed his door and rolled down his window and sighed. I waited a full minute for him to speak while he stared straight ahead. I am getting good at waiting. "God, I'm sorry."

"About what Frank?" My hands were starting to freeze.

He paused again. "About….about your getting fired, about no one standing up for you, about what that shitbird son of mine did at school, about having to suck up, about not knowing Mary, about creating a life and then being a prisoner in it, about the world having gotten to this place. About all of it. I'm just sorry. It's so hard to care about anything because when you do, it just makes you angry and sad when it doesn't work out, and it never works out. Then you go and do what you did, and it makes me feel a little hope, which is almost worse somehow. I thought I'd figured out the world and how to live in it to get by." He looked up at me. "And I'm tired, I guess." I put the casserole down and put my hand on his giant shoulder and gave it a squeeze as best I could.

"Okay. Bye," he said, recovering his composure, and starting his car. "We'll be thinking about you."

I picked up the lasagna and tucked it under one arm and waved. We probably wouldn't see each other again, but he gave me a gift I needed badly. I felt a little better. I sat in my car for a while trying to decide what to do with my freedom. I realized the lasagna would thaw if I didn't get home, so that's where I went.

I called Mary the day it happened, last Thursday, right after I talked to Ernest. I explained what happened and what I had to do. Mary urged then begged me to change my mind. Ten minutes into our conversation, she exploded from the frustration that had probably been building for years. "Life is more than black versus white. We've proved that. We live it. You used to be flexible and understanding, like me, like we all have to be in order to survive. What happened? Why this? You could have written a letter to the editor or something and expressed your disapproval without risking everything. It just isn't that important. What a stupid, stupid thing to make a big deal out of. A flag for God's sake." She stopped for air. I could picture her pacing in the hall, shaking with emotion, picking up things and putting them down. I felt badly I had upset her so much, but I thought she would come around, if not in this conversation then eventually. But my confidence slipped when she continued. "It just doesn't matter. You did this for nothing. You know I don't care about him. I don't know who you are anymore or why I loved you. Now what are we going to do?" she cried and hung up. I drove around a long time before I came home that night, falling into a loneliness so deep it didn't have a bottom. I wanted to tell Mary that surviving wasn't enough, that we all deserved more, but she was already asleep when I got to the bedroom.

Until that Thursday morning, I hadn't thought about Jimmy Holmes for years; he had become less and less relevant with age. Just before the e-mail came, I was looking out the window at the gorgeous grounds of this place. The sun was glinting off of the sculpture garden and the wind made the flags dance. Pat had brought her dog to work; they were the picture of joy playing Frisbee on the grass.

My computer beeped. "Senator Holmes passed away last night," the e-mail began. "All government agencies are directed to lower the State and US flags to half-mast pursuant to Section 7m of the Flag Code, US Code Title 4, Chapter 1, Proclamation 3044 by President Eisenhower, and the Governor's Proclamation of today. If any assistance is needed in understanding or executing these procedures, please call our office." My stomach lurched and panic shot me out of my chair before I knew I had decided what to do. I sprinted three flights downstairs to catch Ernest before he could carry out the order. My heart was pounding furiously when I got to him. He was bent over looking for something on a bottom shelf in his office.

"Ernest, don't even think about it," I panted, my hands planted on his desk.

"Don't think about what sir?" Ernest turned around and looked up but stayed crouched on the floor. He didn't feel my panic. I wished someone would.

"Lowering the flags."

He stood up, with a quizzical look on his face. "But the e-mail....It's what we always do."

"Not this time. Not for this man."

"I don't think we get to pick..."

"I'll take responsibility. Just don't do it. Tell them I threatened your job. I am your boss, right?"

Ernest smiled. "Yes, sir. You always did like to do things your own way, but this is a doozy. Times have changed you know. Are you sure?"

"Ernest, he was a racist who used his power to further that agenda for forty years. To honor that hatemonger is to rewrite history."

"Not really. We're not having a party or anything. It's just a formality." Ernest was trying to placate me.

"Not to me." My heart was still pounding.

"Okay. I won't do it. But someone will."

"No, they won't."

Ernest cocked his head and studied me for a while, then stuck out his hand. I took it with relief and Ernest shook mine so vigorously it hurt my shoulder.

Someone must have overheard us and reported me. Otherwise, it would have taken at least a day for my boss to hear about it. Maybe that would have been enough time to figure something out. But it was all over by late afternoon. The federal marshals watched me clean out my desk and walked me to my car. The sun was low in the sky by then, glinting off the pond, but I could still the flags at half mast through the glare. It was just a symbol, Ernest was right, but for god's sake it's a symbol that means we all join together in honoring that man and his legacy. One of the marshals shook my hand when we got to my car at the far end of the lot, and I was grateful.

It doesn't happen to everyone, but maybe it should: the opportunity to face the one choice that could ruin your life but save your soul. If you're lucky, the choice is so obvious that you feel no emotion, think no thoughts. Mine was. Whatever made me rush downstairs felt chemical, not conscious. I was an athlete in the zone, a priest hearing the voice of God, a fighter pilot dropping a bomb. It was the easiest decision ever; I think it came from some level before decision. Nobody understands why a white man cares that much about an old racist, and I'm not eloquent enough to be able to explain. Those who knew about Mary figured it was because of her, because of what her family went through, when that could not be further from the truth. I felt like a bird trying to justify its migration.

To lower the flags to half-staff for that man's death was not something I could do and still remain who I am. He had done so many horrible, racist things that lowering the flag was a lie, a government supported lie. How could I, a scientist taught to look for the truth, be part of that? How could Mary think I could? If I had gone along, followed the order and put on an agreeable face, I would have split in two. I don't have that much time left to be who I should be, to be whole. I deserved to be fired; I accept that as the consequence of my action. The other consequence, though, losing more of Mary, and maybe the rest of her, was not something I had considered. But then, as I said, I really didn't consider anything.

I did get support from liberal bloggers once my story hit the papers. They wanted to build me a shrine. I was their martyr. They called me a patriot and a moral giant. I was Ghandi, Abraham Lincoln, and Martin Luther King, Jr. all rolled into one. I printed and saved the posts. The right wingers wanted me flayed. Firing wasn't enough; to a person, they wanted me to go to jail for my protest. But within a few days, a new crisis replaced me. A new hero, a new goat. I didn't get my shrine, but I didn't go to jail either.

We preach to our kids that nothing, absolutely nothing, is more important than getting along. We live under the tyranny of nice. Smile and shake the devil's hand or else you're the bad guy. Lower the flag for the senator because his status deserves respect. Everything is relative, so don't judge. But judgments are necessary, unless you just want to float down the river like a rotten log, your beliefs replaced by air. Some things are unforgiveable. Once done they cannot be zeroed out by placing good deeds on the other side of the scale. These unforgivable things, these actions or opinions, are different for everyone. We may not even be conscious of what they are until we face that choice. I found out what mine are, before it was too late. I guess that may be all I get out of life.

Mary is different. She doesn't have to act on what she believes. She doesn't lose herself every time she has to do or say something she doesn't agree with. She says she doesn't want to live like her parents did, fighting all the time. She says being pragmatic and ignoring the worst of the world is how she learned to survive. I understand that. But more and more, that trait has turned her into mush. Hate and love, action and calm, judgment and acceptance are all pairs that need their opposites.

"Holmes was a racist," I reminded her in that phone conversation last week.

"So? He's dead. You didn't do anything or change anything or save anybody. You just lost your job and someone else lowered the flags."

"I showed the world, or at least our part of it, that racism matters, even to me, a white man."

"Exactly. A white man. You're not black," she reminded me. "Why not let us pick our own battles?"

I was horrified, and she could tell. "I didn't mean it that way. You are so damn sensitive." She spat the words at me. My silence continued, so she filled it. "None of this can be undone. It was a whim, a grand, selfish melodramatic gesture. Everyone has a boss. Why did you think you didn't? You had to know you'd lose your job. You were looking for a way out, that must be it. You're having a late mid-life crisis."

"His life was spent fighting against justice, against human rights. He was evil. How could I honor that man and still love you?"

"Is that why you love me? Because I'm black? Does it make you feel better? You know, it's not about what some senator did or didn't do or about loving me. It's about you and your need to be noble, to be noticed, to sacrifice something. I don't know why you picked this as the vehicle, but that's all it is, a vehicle. For what, I don't know."

She hasn't really talked to me since that phone call. I had thought she would be proud of me. But at least she hasn't left. As I recalled her words for the hundredth time today, I thought for the first time that maybe she is partially right, that I was looking for a way out. Maybe I knew at some level I needed a crisis, and this was the first one to come along that fit. I still think it was more than that, that it was a magical, pure, selfless act, but maybe not. Maybe it was both. It has certainly exposed the fault lines.

What's left of my hair has gotten much grayer over the past week. I look exhausted, but I feel spry, ready to run a marathon. It's a strange mix of contradictory images and sensations every time I look in the mirror. I look in the mirror a lot lately, sometimes for up to an hour when Mary's out, trying to reconcile the images with my feelings. I see nakedness when I look at my face, and I like it. I wish Mary liked what she saw. I wonder how she feels when she looks at her face, the face she arranges to suit so many other people. Is she whole, is she happy? Shouldn't we know that about each other when we're old as well as when we're young?

I did what I needed to do and paid a price. Mary thought I was wrong. It's deeper than that, but it also isn't. Let's move on and see what's around the corner, I've wanted to say to her. There must be parts of us left that we love. But the time has never felt right. I need to stop.

Mary's car rolls up on our gravel driveway. She's been waging a campaign to have it paved. The kids are grown, so her argument that it would be good for a basketball hoop doesn't make much sense. I think she's just tired of pulling weeds out of it, plus the edges are ragged, not neat like the rest of the manicured yard. I think the gravel softens the otherwise severe look of the yard with all its geometric beds and trimmed and plucked vegetation. And I love the way her car sounds pulling up on the rocks. It makes my heart leap, even now when I know there is a gulf between us so wide we may not be able to cross it. A car on pavement doesn't sound like it is coming home. I probably wouldn't even hear it. Gravel makes me happy. It makes her unhappy. That's our marriage in a nutshell lately. I'll win this one by default, though; we'll need to avoid unnecessary expenses.

I righted the lamp and the trashcan and turned the computer on. Mary turned the key in the lock out of habit I guess, since she must have seen my car. I heard her come in and the slap of the mail landing on the hall table. Her footsteps left the marble of the entry and stopped on the hall carpet.

"Bill?"

"In here." I moved a few papers around on the desk to make some working noises. I'm supposed to be job hunting, not wasting time thinking about killing myself.

Mary reached her head around the door frame, the symbolism of which was not lost on me. Lately, she can't fully enter any room where I am. I'm not sure she's even aware of it. Her coat hung open, and I saw that she had put the lining in it.

"I got lamb chops for dinner. On sale." She pulled her head back around the corner and headed for the kitchen where I heard her unloading groceries.

"Sounds great. Any other bags in the car?" I remembered to ask, raising my voice so she could hear me.

"No, thanks though."

I got up, put my sock and shoe back on and shut the closet door.

"I saw Joyce at the grocery store."

I waited for the rest, but any more seemed to require my presence. This first conversation wasn't going to come easy, but I wanted it badly. I tied my shoe and walked down the hall, through the great room and into the kitchen. We redesigned the kitchen a few years ago. I still remember our debates over countertops. It all seemed a little extravagant to me at the time, but the granite does look nice.

Mary was in the middle of putting a bag of apples into the refrigerator's lower drawer when I came into her line of sight. I don't make loud footsteps in these shoes. I waited for a few minutes.

"It's starting to rain," I offered.

"It's supposed to rain the rest of the week," Mary said.

"I should check the gutters."

"We had those guards put in last year, remember? They should be fine."

"How was Joyce?" I asked.

Mary retuned to the counter and continued to empty her purchases. I waited, because it seemed the least I could do, and I was good at it. She finally stopped with one hand still in the bag and spoke without looking at me.

"She said she cut out the *Herald's* story on what you did and made a laminated copy for each of her kids. She said to tell you thank you." The way she was hunched over, talking to the bag, let me see the back of her neck. Mary looked up at me and half smiled, like she was waiting to see if that was enough. I kissed her on the cheek and helped her put away the rest of the food.

"Will you turn on NPR?" Mary asked, setting the lamb chops on the broiler pan and rubbing them with spices.

"Sure." I reached up to the radio on top of the refrigerator and switched it on. "I'll be back in a minute. Should I get some wine?"

"That would be nice."

I walked back to the study and sat in my chair for a while looking out of the window. It has a great view of the river. I should probably just get rid of the gun.

RAW MATERIALS

"Your Dad's been dead a year now. You don't think your mother knows? I mean she must have some connection with the outside world besides you." Brad poured two cups of coffee, put milk in his and passed Carla hers.

"I don't know. Maybe she heard, but I doubt it. She cut all her old ties. Everything not on the island is dead to her." Carla hadn't spoken to her mother in two years, not since her father got sick. It wasn't entirely on purpose; it was just the way things worked out.

"That can't be true," Brad chided her. "She sends us Christmas cards. So we're not dead."

Carla shrugged. Christmas cards were proof of nothing. Certainly not love. And what did Brad know anyway, she thought. His childhood was like a Norman Rockwell painting made into a Disney movie. His parents were still married and living in the same house he grew up in; it even had a real white picket fence that Brad whitewashed in the summers for his allowance. His family vacationed at the beach; they didn't try and move there.

Her parents, on the other hand, yanked Carla out of school and away from everything she knew and moved her to the island when she was eight. It was her mother's fantasy to live off the land and never be cold again. She had sacrificed a lot to put Carla's father through medical school, so after a few years of work and a good nest egg in the bank, he felt he could let her indulge her fantasy for a couple of years. They owed her, he told Carla when she kept asking him why they had to leave.

Jo – she shortened her name from Josephine the minute they landed on the island, shedding the extra syllables with the same joy with which she dropped off her coats and sweaters at Goodwill – always hated the winter. It hated her back, giving her scaly skin, hat hair, asthma and black moods. The island was her idea of heaven. Carla's dad only lasted three years before he was ready to return to real life and his medical practice. He realized that he needed more than sand and sun and water and fish to feed his soul. But Jo refused to leave. Their grand lark of an experiment had become her life, and she liked it. She explained in as many different ways as she could to Carla that she had found her place and her purpose and finally felt whole and how important that was to a woman, and how rare. But Carla wasn't terribly interested in her mother's explanations. When her parents divorced, Carla was happy to go with her father. He tried to make up for any hurt Carla felt by giving her every possible opportunity. They travelled, they went to the theatre and concerts, and he sent her to camps and got her horseback riding lessons when she asked. All those experiences gave her an appreciation for the variety the right life can offer. She learned that she liked having options and choices and felt lucky to know that about herself at an early age.

Carla knew she should have called her mother for the funeral. But she was angry, and when she stopped being angry she was sad. When she stopped being sad, she was busy. It didn't matter anyway, Carla thought. She would make up for it now. And her mother, for all her flaws, didn't hold a grudge.

Brad picked up the remote and turned on the morning news. He sipped his coffee quietly until they got to the weather.

"It looks like you shouldn't have any problems with your flights if you can get out of Kennedy. It's all clear south of us."

"That's good news." The rain in New York had been going on for days. It would be nice to see the sun, Carla thought. And she loved flying. It was the one time she didn't have to do anything else or be anywhere else. She could think.

"Do you have everything you need?" Brad was pouring granola for both of them.

"I could use some courage."

"Why?" Brad stopped on his way to the refrigerator for milk and looked at her, confused.

She really didn't know why she hadn't told him. When it came to her mother, or lately Brad too she realized with a pinch of fear, she often didn't know why she did or didn't do things. It was like her own thoughts were written in a language she couldn't read.

"I'm going to ask her to come back and live here. We can get her an apartment in the city. Or on Long Island if she would rather be near the ocean."

Brad just stared at her. "Why?" He repeated.

"I don't know."

"Seriously? How could you not know the answer to something like that?"

"Look, she is old. She can't stay there forever. The ocean is rising. The last time I was there, the high tide almost came up to her garden. Her house could be gone soon. All the islands in the chain are going to be underwater in fifty years."

"Well, she'll be dead way before then. Plus lots of old people live on that island."

Brad had gone with her on a visit once years ago. He thought it was hot and boring and full of old people. Which it was, but it made Carla sad that she couldn't show him the good parts. She didn't know if it was her fault or his. And there were good parts, she had always known that. They just weren't good enough.

"I mean damnit, I don't have room for anything else in my life. Neither do you, for that matter. Your mother loves that island. You say that all the time. It would kill her to leave. I thought you were only going for a visit. Jeez, I wish you wouldn't flake out on me like this just when things were going so smoothly."

Carla had thought she was just going for a visit, and maybe the last one, but over the past weeks, things started to shift in her mind, and she kept revisiting her past. She knew it was partially because she was between projects and had energy and brain space to spare, but that knowledge didn't stop the confusing thoughts. She needed to make them stop before she went crazy from the chaos. She was starting to understand how people must feel when they hear voices.

"Maybe you should see somebody again," Brad suggested.

Carla ignored him, even though she agreed with him. It bothered her that she and so many of her friends in New York needed therapy to get through their lives. New York seemed to be built on a foundation of service people who could soothe, cleanse, and buff all the rough edges off your life so you could fit into whatever slot you had chosen for yourself. She tried not to think about it.

Instead she thought back to her first return trip to the island. It was fifteen years ago, right after college. Carla needed a break after a bad relationship, and her father encouraged her to go to the island. She fought him, saying she never wanted to see her mother again, but he insisted, paid for the ticket and even bought her a nice camera to take along.

"Hide behind that. If you need to get out of the house, just say you're going to take pictures," he had said, winking.

The camera changed everything. It brought her closer to the island and its beauty and peace and for a brief time to her mother. Carla spent six months there and returned every year for the next ten. Behind the camera, she felt safe. From that perch she could be a visitor, a recorder, not a part of the place. She was better able to love things like that. From a distance.

When she got back from that post-college trip, she showed the photos to her father who showed them to a friend and so on until they reached an art dealer acquaintance who loved them. Those photos of the island and its people and her mother's motley group of friends shot her to stardom in a New York art world hungry for a new photography star. One of the early reviewers wrote: "The unschooled Thompson's portraits, particularly those of fisherman readying their boats for the day, tell us less about individual people than about the worlds they inhabit, which is perhaps the main truth of the best portraits. She is a worthy heir to Arbus, albeit one who uses color to great effect where Arbus preferred the gritty grays, and Thompson makes the natural world a lively character in her portraits, adding a new layer to the Arbus style. They are simply stunning."

Elton John had bought one of the first series, and so had Hillary Clinton. That was all it took. Carla went back the next year and the next and started experimenting with different equipment. One year she took a large format Polaroid camera with her; on another trip she took a pinhole camera. Now she made a comfortable living taking pictures, doing what she loved. She had an apartment in Chelsea that was the envy of her friends, and a boyfriend who ran a charter school and believed in making a difference in the world. She had it all.

The story she told herself about why she had stopped travelling to the island was that she needed to refresh herself creatively. The truth was that her mother was growing more exasperating and her relationship with Brad becoming more serious. At the same time, Carla found a new passion photographing people on subway platforms. The work didn't sell as well; people like blue in their photographs Sarabeth told her. (Sarabeth was her favorite gallerist.) But it was close to home and important, Carla thought. There is something about people travelling that we need to stop and look at. People in their lives are one thing; people on the way to their lives are something else. That distinction fascinated Carla, and she didn't know why everyone else couldn't see it.

Brad's voice startled her. "If you want a relationship with her, make one. Visit more. I'll even go with you. Don't be so dramatic. She'll never move. You know that."

She forgot they were having a fight. "Maybe not." Carla didn't say anything else. She knew Brad would soon tire of arguing with her even though he was good at it. She finished packing, and then they grabbed a taxi to the airport. They shared a kiss, some words about missing each other, and then Brad headed for the subway home. Carla could be alone with her thoughts.

She killed the ninety minutes in the airport with a cup of frozen yogurt and a trip through all the shops. She got to the gate just as they announced boarding. She waited her turn, shuffled to her seat and found homes for her backpack and duffel bag. Take off went without a hitch, and everything seemed to go smoothly for a while until the plane hit a patch of turbulence so violent and sudden it made her stomach flip. It's the loss of control, one of her friends said when Carla mentioned how much she hated turbulence. Your work is all about control, he continued. No it's not, Carla had protested. I shoot what I see. Ivan insisted he meant technically, that Carla controlled the camera, the lighting, the printing, the whole universe of art making. Carla accepted that. So long as no one accused her of controlling the subjects. They were doing what they did naturally when she photographed them. Her presence made no difference. She was invisible.

Carla realized that her seatmate was talking. She swallowed her sigh and removed her headphones. Turbulence made some people chatty.

"Excuse me?" she responded as politely as she could.

"I said will this be your first time visiting Barbados?"

"No, I've been many times," Carla answered.

"Ooh, lucky you! This is my first time. Have you ever been to The Flying Fish?"

That resort is overpriced and abuses its staff, Carla wanted to answer. But more than telling the truth, she didn't want to get involved. "It's lovely. I'm sure you'll have a wonderful time," she said, sliding her headphones back on with a smile and a nod that she hoped was accepted as the polite exit she needed it to be.

The woman seemed to understand but briefly looked hurt. Carla felt bad, but knew it was better that she got out of the conversation before she did or said anything more hurtful. She seemed to possess a special talent for hurting the feelings of middle-aged women.

They had three hours left in the flight. Carla would make it up to her as they got closer to the end. She turned up the volume on the Spanish guitar music her guitar teacher had recommended and tried to identify the chords. Brad had suggested she learn a musical instrument when she went though her last period of 'creative constipation' as another of her gallerists called it. Brad said the concentration required to learn an instrument would free up her subconscious creative mind to come up with new ideas for her work. Or something like that. They used music in much of the curriculum at his school, so Brad had a lot of confidence in its power. Carla wasn't very good at the guitar, but she did like the way she would sometimes lose herself when she practiced. Practicing did bounce her out of her creative drought, partly because her frustration with her inability to make her fingers hit the right notes without eyeing them like a hawk forced her back to the camera where everything was easier.

She gave up on the chord identification game and pulled out her sketchbook. While she never posed the photos she took, she did keep a journal of scenes she imagined and then looked for. How else would she know something was special, she would say to her critics. She didn't believe in working intuitively and thought people who said they did were just lazy. Her mother, however, would say that Carla just didn't have any faith in her intuition. This trip should prove Jo wrong about that.

While Carla sketched, she thought about the dream. She couldn't help it. She rarely had dreams. A former therapist said that she probably dreamt every night like most people, she just didn't remember them. Carla knew that was wrong. This recent dream was the same one she had as a child every night for a year after leaving the island. She had never dreamed that dream or a single other one in all the intervening years. In it, a tsunami came and washed everyone and everything off the island. But the people were all able to swim back safely. And in that way of dreams, the buildings reappeared, dry and undamaged. The only change after the water left was that the island had a new population of fish that could walk. The walking fish took over everything, leaving the people starving and homeless. It must mean something, and because Carla didn't know what other meaning the dream could have, she figured it meant she needed to save her mother. If not from walking fish, from something aquatic. You don't have to like somebody to want to save them, she told herself.

More turbulence shook the plane and the flight attendant's voice urged the passengers to fasten their seatbelts at the captain's request. Carla was pretty sure the captain didn't give a damn whether anyone fastened their seatbelt, but the flight attendants knew no one would listen to them without some backup authority. Carla always left hers fastened, so she finished her water in case the plastic cup went flying and tried to keep sketching. While she was going to be back on that island, she might as well try and take some good shots. She only packed her workaday SLR, but she still figured she could get something. Sarabeth had been hounding her for more island photos for the gallery anyway.

Carla had been working on a series in McDonald's play structures which she loved, but it wasn't selling as well as even the subway photos. She didn't know why. She loved the contrast between the bright colors and happy children and the exhausted parents. The McDonald's photos were mean, Sarabeth had said. "You can tell you don't like anyone or anything in the pictures. You can tell you're laughing, exposing people. People want to buy love. It's okay if the picture is ugly, but they have to believe there is love behind it. Or hope. People love to buy hope. Go back to your island. Find some hope."

Carla hadn't told Brad about that conversation either.

As usual when she worked, Carla lost complete track of time; only when her bladder urged her to get up did she look at her watch. They would be landing in an hour. The turbulence hadn't gone away, but it had subsided enough to become background jiggling. She opened the window screen to see the ocean. Carla loved seeing the ocean from above and often tried unsuccessfully to photograph it. It turned out she needed people in her photos to make them any good.

She excused herself and stepped gingerly over her seatmate's feet and purse on her way to the bathroom. When she came back, her seatmate had pulled out her brochures.

"How long will you be staying," asked Carla, giving in to the inevitable.

"Two weeks! My sister is coming for the second week, but she couldn't get as much vacation time as I did. Where will you be staying?"

"I'm actually headed to a different island. I'll get on a small plane and then a ferry."

"Oh, how exciting and remote! Is there a resort there, or will you be camping or something fun like that?"

Carla debated quickly how much to reveal. "I'm visiting a friend who's doing research." It was true enough. Jo kept records of everything she saw, so what was that if not research?

"Is your friend working on global warming? I hear some of the little outer islands won't be around much longer with rising ocean levels."

"Sort of."

"It's so sad, isn't it?"

"Yes, it is sad."

"I'm just glad I get to see this area before it disappears. I mean I know that sounds selfish. . ."

"It's okay. We're all selfish," Carla said. She was feeling suddenly generous. "Beautiful places are good for the soul."

The irony that made Carla smile inside was that her mother's island – not that her mother owned it, that is just how Carla always thought of it – was not particularly beautiful. Brad liked to call it the land of the misfit toys. The original inhabitants were almost outnumbered by damaged people who came to the island by accident or to hide from their past lives. The west side of the island had been used as a shooting range by the U.S. Navy and still looked blasted even though the Navy stopped using it forty years ago.

She leaned back and closed her eyes and let herself think of Leroy for the first time all day. She wondered if he would be happy to see her after all these years. Leroy was the first outsider to join the huge, mismatched family her mother eventually assembled. All living things gravitated to Jo and flourished. It had been that way when they lived in Boston, but on the island she had room for more and no other obligations or seasonal depression to hold her back. Carla was nine and Leroy looked about eleven when he showed up without a last name, or at least without one he was willing to confess. Instead of pushing him, Jo asked him to take a week and then pick a new one. He picked Shakespeare, thanks, Carla assumed, to the multi volume "Complete Works of William Shakespeare" in the guest bedroom he was given. Carla and Leroy became best friends and went everywhere together. Leroy taught her how to surf and fish and she taught him how to draw and lie. Neither of them were very good students, but that didn't stop them from forging the kind of deep connection only lonely children can. Carla's father loved him too and tried to take him with them when they left, but Leroy would have none of it. The island was the only home he ever knew and he was fiercely loyal to Jo.

He was what Carla missed most about the island as a child and young adult, and on that fateful trip back after college they fell into an intense but brief love affair. It ended when she left, and they never slept together again after that summer, but she thought they stayed friends. He always drove her around to take her photographs and they talked about their lives.

"Ladies and gentlemen, we are beginning our descent. Please check the security of your seatbelts, return all seats and tray tables to the upright and locked position and stow any personal belongings you may have used during the flight. We'll be on the ground in twenty minutes."

When the plane landed, Carla helped her seatmate find the hotel shuttle, stood still for an uncomfortable hug and then headed to the general aviation building for her flight. She rode with the mail to the next island in the chain and then got in line for the ferry to her mother's island. The ferry captain recognized her and brought her a beer which put her in a much better frame of mind. Everyone with any connection to her mother got special treatment, especially Carla, even though people knew they didn't get along particularly well.

Jo was there at the dock to meet her along with three of the dogs she always collected. Carla thought she recognized the one with the gray face.

"Leroy's married," she said. That was how her mother liked to deliver news, the way other people would pull off a bandaid. Carla stumbled; the news hit like a two by four to the back of her head, and the impact made her feel faint.

"You still love him."

How could she know? Carla didn't know until just now. And she wasn't going to let her mother know she was right. She swallowed a few times and bent down to get her water bottle from her luggage. She took a drink and replaced it.

"Is that Eggplant?" Carla asked when she stood up, cupping the dog's chin and looking into his friendly eyes.

"Yup."

"Wow. He must be . . . fifteen?"

"Something like that. I was never sure how old he was when he came sniffing around the house, hungry as a teenage boy." Jo seemed willing to play along.

They walked to her mother's house. It was the same as Carla remembered. Yellow painted cinderblock with a giant chain link fence and a mismatched but ridiculously fertile garden framed by a new white picket fence. The new fence was plastic, like so many things on the island, but still it was a nice effect. Carla upgraded from feeling faint to feeling dizzy.

"How do you grow things so well in this sandy soil?" Carla asked, using words to pull herself together.

"Dog pee," her mother said, and chuckled. "How long are you staying?"

"Four days."

"Okay." If anything, Jo was too easygoing.

The house smelled good to Carla; she hadn't remembered that. They had snapper and conch and salad and bread for dinner. Ice cream for dessert. They always had ice cream for dessert.

"Did you hear about Dad?" Carla asked after dinner.

"Yeah."

"Why didn't you call or come to the funeral?"

"We've been divorced for years. We had already mourned the loss of each other. Death didn't add or take anything away. Why didn't you call me?"

"I was angry."

"So what's new? You've always been angry at me."

"I guess I don't know then. How did you find out?"

"Leroy keeps in touch with my sister."

"Oh."

Just hearing his name hurt again in a small but deep way, like a needle going into her forehead. Carla didn't know how many punctures she could take. She suddenly wished she hadn't come and got a sinking feeling in her stomach that things were going to get worse.

"I'm going to bed. Did you bring your camera?" her mother asked.

"Just the SLR."

"Okay, then. Goodnight."

Carla sat at the table for a long time after her mother left.

The next day, Leroy was in the kitchen when Carla came out of her bedroom for coffee. She saw him before he saw her. She stopped and looked at him. His skin was still so beautifully and deeply black, like patent leather. He had a way of standing that made you want to sit. Carla felt her knees go a little weak. It had been seven years, and those years were kinder to his looks than they had been to hers. That made her a little angry, and the anger gave her enough strength to walk in without betraying her soul.

Her mother was making pancakes.

"Welcome back, Carla. I came to drive you around today if you like. To take pictures," Leroy said. They must have been talking about her because he looked uncomfortable. He never looked uncomfortable. Leroy either already possessed whatever natural equilibrium Jo had, or he learned it from her. They were a pair, Carla had to admit.

"Okay. Thanks."

Somehow, they all ate together. Jo talked non stop about the latest government scandal and her attempts to hybridize the strains of lavender she loved and a million other things Carla let wash over her. She was grateful for the soundtrack.

"Your mom had me paint the truck purple," Leroy said when they climbed in after doing the dishes. "She wanted it to look like the sky after sunset when a storm is coming."

"That's more of an inky blue."

"Not here. Remember?"

Carla closed her eyes and tried to remember. "I guess not. So when do I get to meet her?"

Leroy gripped the wheel and then let go. "I was hoping I would get to tell you."

"That would have been nice." Carla reflexively crossed her arms to protect herself.

"I'm sorry. If we had kept in touch. . ."

"If we had kept in touch? What does that mean? We would have had a shot? Would you have come to New York? I would never come back here."

"I know. I meant I would have told you about her when I met her." Leroy pulled over and stopped the truck. "Do you want to walk for a minute? I cannot talk about this and drive."

"Fine."

They got out and crossed the road to where the shoulder was wider.

"I did love you. Very much. More than you were capable of loving me or anyone at that time. Why do you think I was always around? But that love died. It had to. You stopped loving the island and then me. I think we were the same to you. It became about you, about work, about what you could take. I could tell. So I do not carry a torch for you."

Carla closed her eyes and winced.

"Why does that make you sad?"

She forgot how honest Leroy could be, how his questions could pull the truth out of a person.

"I guess I wish I could have kept loving you. I wish I could cut out whatever was in the way of loving you, of loving this place, hell, of loving my mother. It's like there is a giant rock that is covering the door to a cellar I am trapped in. I don't know when it showed up or what I did to invite it in. It is just getting bigger. But I do not feel it when I am not here. That is why I stopped coming, and I guess that is why I am unhappy."

"Then this is not a good place for you. Or no, maybe it is the best place for you. Maybe you have to learn to push the rock away. I do not know."

"Tell me about her."

Leroy made circles in the sand with the toe of his shoe for a long time before answering her.

"Dinah came to the island as a substitute vet to see to the government's cattle. You mother asked her to look at one of the dogs. I don't think there was anything wrong with the dog – she just wanted us to meet."

That detail hurt her as much as him getting married. Her mother had given up on her. Of course, she hadn't really given her any option.

"She went back to the big island after a few days and we took turns visiting. But she loved it here, so she moved her practice and is now the local vet. Watching her with animals, it's like she is a witch. I was drawn to her. And she loves me, too."

"Well that's the way it should be, right?"

Leroy just nodded, as if embarrassed to have so much in front of someone who had so little.

"Why do you still work for my mother?"

"She makes me laugh. And there is not much other work here," Leroy confessed.

Carla never could figure out how her mother made enough money not only to live, but to have employees.

"We don't need much here," Leroy said, answering her unspoken question.

"I guess that is why I didn't fit in," Carla said. "I need a lot."

"You want a lot. There's a difference. Do you know what you need?"

"I thought I did. Now, I am not so sure. I just know something has been dying in me for a long time and I haven't noticed it until now. That's scary."

Leroy changed the subject. Even he couldn't go some places. "What do you want to shoot?" This was their routine every time she came. Their safe place.

"Can we go to the windward side and check out the cafes?"

"Sure." Leroy started the truck and Carla got in.

He parked along the road and read while she took pictures. When she was done, she got back in the truck and they headed home.

"Do you like New York?" Leroy asked.

"Yes, of course. It's the greatest city in the world. There is always something to do and see, things to stimulate me creatively. It's a wonderful place."

"Then why are you here?"

"People take vacations to visit family."

"This is not a vacation."

"Now you are just being mean," Carla said, feeling caught in a trap. She didn't want to tell him about the dream, and now she was confused about why she came back anyway. She didn't like being confused; she was never confused in New York.

"I am sorry. I am just interested in you. I always have been. Ever since we were kids. It was like you had a secret."

"You were the one with the secret, coming out of the blue with no past."

"I guess so. But you had a different secret. One you kept from yourself."

"So now you're the island mystic and I'm the cold city bitch?" Carla forgot her earlier confessions.

"You are not a bitch. You are just confused."

"Fuck you. Why do you care?"

"You are a part of my past. A special part. And your mother cares, and I care about her."

"It's that simple?"

"Yes. For me most things are."

They passed a church that Carla used to photograph. It was crumbling now. The congregation had built a new, bigger church that was utterly unphotographable.

"Do you know what you believe in?" Leroy asked her.

"Like what kind of god? No, I'm an atheist." Was she? Carla wasn't sure, but she didn't spend much time on the issue. Brad called himself an agnostic. That was a coward's word, she had always thought without telling him.

"No, like love or laughter or art."

"You can't believe or not believe in that stuff. It just is," Carla said.

"Belief is about things that are. That exist. You just put them in a hierarchy that matters to you."

"That's not belief."

"I think it is," said Leroy.

"Good for you." Carla was angry.

"Well, what matters to you then?"

"Lots of stuff." She felt out of place here. She felt like a loser in some cosmic game, and she was not used to losing. At least not lately. They rode the rest of the way back to her mother's house in silence.

"Thanks for the ride," Carla said when they got there.

"You're welcome. I am sorry I made you upset."

"That's okay," Carla lied. "I think I'm always upset." That much was true, she realized. It had become her normal state.

She went inside, and Leroy drove off. Her mother was out, but the dogs were happy to see Carla, so she took them outside one by one and brushed their coats. She set up her camera after the first one and using the self-timer took photos of herself with the dogs as proof she was there. And as proof of something else she couldn't define.

When her mother came back loaded with bags from the market, Carla had recovered herself and decided she had better bring up her plan.

"Mom, would you ever consider moving back to the states?" Beating around the bush was a waste of time with her mother.

"Which one?"

"Mine. New York."

"No. Why? I love it here."

Carla had nothing left but the dream card, and she played it.

"Mom, I had a dream, and I never have dreams. I think. . ."

"Was it about the walking fish again?"

Carla just stared, gape-mouthed. Some on the island thought she was the first white woman to have the third eye and a healing touch.

"How could you know?"

"You forget I was there for every minute of your first eleven years. There are things I remember." Jo went to the bookshelf in the living room and pulled out a tattered and flimsy but thick paperback with an orange cover. "This was a book we got at the big island." She handed it to Carla.

Carla flipped through the pages. Each chapter was introduced with a black and white drawing of a big wave washing the people off an island and fish with feet populating the empty shops and roads.

"So it wasn't a vision."

"Nope. Just a memory all tangled up with a child's fears. It was either the best book we ever bought for you or the worst.

You woke up with nightmares for weeks. But at least you engaged with it. It was the first time we shared something after we moved here. I'm sorry to burst your bubble, Carla."

"I just thought that I had a way in, that's all."

"A way in to what?"

"To you, to this."

"Carla, the way in has always been there, you just don't want it. You don't need a dream vision to be able to talk to me. You've always been looking for a way out anyway."

"But it isn't safe here. The ocean. . ."

"Yeah, the ocean is rising. But it is still glorious here for now, and it is my home. I love the water and the people and my dogs and the life I have built. I'm not going anywhere. I'm at peace."

"So I am just supposed to go home and wait for news that you are dead?"

"You could stay here. You loved this place once. You can love it again. People here love you." Mom nodded out the window to Leroy who was tying up the boat.

"Not you."

"Just because I chose to stay here doesn't mean I didn't love you."

"It did to a child."

"I am sorry. I had hoped you would get over that."

Carla could not accept her mother's apology. "This is not a fight you can win, Mom."

"This is not a fight at all."

"Yes, it is."

"Look, I have always told you the truth. Shown you the truth. Lived the damn truth. You just haven't listened. You run from whatever you don't want to be true."

"Well, I'm not running now."

"But you will."

Carla looked at her mother with disbelief. Jo looked back. The truck drove up and Leroy came back and stood in the kitchen doorway. He looked at the two of them until Carla couldn't stand it anymore. She got up and went into her room, coming out in a sports bra and her running shorts with goggles in her hand. "I'm going for a swim."

"I'll go with you," Leroy said. "The water is not like you remember it."

"I'll be fine," Carla said and stalked off.

It was a hot walk to the beach, and Carla wished she had shoes. But she wasn't going back. As soon as she got past the breakers, she felt all her problems wash away. It had been so long since she had swum in a pool, much less the ocean. She forgot how buoyant and free she was in the warm salt water. And the water was so clear that she could see the fish swimming twenty feet under her. She swam parallel to the shore for a while, trying not to think about her mother. Trying just to let the water embrace her. She found a rhythm in her stroke and felt like she could swim forever. Then a cormorant landed right in front of her and startled her out of her reverie. She looked up and saw she was far down the beach. Rip current, she thought, that's why the swimming was so easy. Shit. She turned over on her back to save energy and could feel she was being pulled out. She knew to wait it out and then swim to shore once the current released her, but she was so far out already she started to panic. She calmed herself down and rolled back over and did some breaststroke, relying on her powerful legs. She used the water tower as a focal point. When she realized the current had relaxed and she was making some progress, she switched to freestyle, put her head down and fought for shore.

The sun was setting when she finally touched land. Her mother and Leroy were there with the truck. She was angry at them for watching her. She was the one who watched. But she was too tired to be angry for long, and she was grateful for the ride.

They drove home in silence. Everyone smiled and waved as her mother drove by.

"It's the purple. It makes people happy," Jo said in what seemed like an apology.

"No, mom," Carla said with her eyes closed and offered her own. "You do."

"Everyone but you."

"I guess that has to be okay for both of us."

On the flight back, Carla slept but had horrible dreams. She was afraid she had lost her mind, that half of it had split off and stayed on the island.

Brad was outside baggage claim with a taxi.

"Welcome home, babe! Whoa, you look tan and sexy."

"Thanks."

"All alone?"

"Yeah. She has no interest in coming."

"Your mother is a crazy old bat. You – we – are better off without her. Come on, let's focus on our work and our life. What we can do here to change the world. Right?"

She smiled and Brad held the door of the taxi.

At home, he made her a drink.

"Worrying about her was keeping you from working. And there is nothing you could do. You know that." Brad rattled the ice cubes in his scotch glass. "It's over now, right?" He wouldn't look at her.

"I guess so."

"Did you bring anything back with you?"

"No." Carla lied.

"I bet you at least got some good pictures."

Carla shrugged. She thought she did, she thought the ones of her and the dogs might be the best pictures of her life, but she didn't know if she would ever show them. To Brad or to anyone.

INSTEAD

As he had every day for the last five, Henry Middleton watched her walk down the school steps and across the parking lot to her car, an old, banana yellow Toyota Celica.

Henry was the new principal at Red Rock Middle School. Celine had been the nurse at Red Rock for the past ten years. On his tour the first day, his assistant principal, Veronica White, told him Celine was trouble and that the parents didn't like her. She didn't mind her own business and she overstepped her boundaries, they said. But Henry liked what he saw of Celine as they passed the nurse's office that first day.

"There, there, Jesse," she cooed as she mopped the blood running down his shin.

"I want my mommy," the boy wailed.

"Your mommy's working sweetie. She'll be there when you get home, but now, you have to be a little man and take one for the team."

"What team?" Jesse was still crying, so his words came out in a wet, breathy stutter.

"The team you and your mother and your little sister make. A family is like a team. One little skinned knee isn't enough to make your mother take time off work. You'll be fine. I'll be your temporary mommy until you feel better."

Jesse sniffed and let Celine tend to his cut.

Every school Henry had ever worked at was divided between those who sided with the principal and those who didn't. Henry hoped he could make an ally of Celine, without causing trouble with Veronica, who he was realizing he didn't like very much. He actually hoped for a lot more with Celine, but he didn't dare focus on that. Not now anyway, he had to get home. Friday night bridge was sacred, and Henry's role as chauffer to his aging mother was the main reason he had moved to Phoenix.

So Henry slipped the file he was reading into his briefcase and snapped it shut. Then he put his forehead briefly on the smooth black leather to gather strength from its coolness. The air conditioning hadn't worked right since he got here. He lifted his head and then his body out of the chair with what felt like the biggest effort of his life. He wanted to stay there until Monday morning when Celine came to work at 8 o'clock. Instead, and it seemed lately that every thing he did felt like it was instead of something he really wanted to do, he grabbed his jacket from the back of the door and headed to his car.

Stepping into the bleaching sunlight, Henry could see that Celine was squatting next to her front passenger tire. He walked over.

"It's flat," she said as he approached.

"I see that. May I call someone for you?"

"Who, a magic fairy? Ghostbusters?"

"No, um well, AAA or a tow truck?"

"I figured Mr. Principal. I was just trying to see if you laughed. I can manage just fine, thank you. I have a jack and a spare tire and a strong back. I do appreciate you stopping, though."

Celine went to her truck and reached in next to the driver's seat to pull the lever and pop the trunk open. Henry stood there, irritated, embarrassed and excited all at once. He'd been dismissed, but he was actually talking to her and he was not going to give up.

"Mind if I watch, then? I could use a refresher course on changing a tire." He smiled and sat on his briefcase.

"Celine lowered the trunk and looked at Henry. "Mr. Principal."

"Call me Henry."

"Henry," she paused, "I think this year will be fun."

BORDER CROSSING

"What are you doing?"

Kate would never have heard the question if she hadn't turned off her hedge trimmer for a few seconds to evaluate her work. She was supposed to wear ear protection, but she rarely did. She actually liked the noise, finding it peaceful. The smell was another matter, although the effectiveness of the gasoline's assault on her system was lessening with daily exposure.

With a gloved hand she shielded her eyes from the glare of the late summer sun and looked out from her three story perch next to the old sycamore. Nothing. I better not be hearing things, Kate thought, shaking her head. Bending over the safety railing on each side of the square platform, Kate was relieved on the fourth bend to locate a child almost directly underneath the lift.

"Um, hi," Kate said.

"Hello!" The tiny girl swung her hand over her head like she was hailing a cab or trying to scare grackles out of a garden. To be fair, it was hard to tell if the girl looked tiny because she was tiny or because she was far away. Kate's artistic training taught her that being thirty feet above something changes perspective a lot more than being thirty feet away from it on flat ground. Colors, though, were unaffected by vertical or horizontal distance. And the girl was brightly colored.

"Trimming the trees," Kate finally answered.

"Why?"

Oh boy here we go, thought Kate. She grimaced and rubbed her neck. One why would spawn another and another the way a single graffiti tag multiplied into a solid wall of chaotic color. What was it called in high school biology? Asexual reproduction. All of a sudden there would be a thousand amoebas. If she answered the starter question, it would be why, why, why, why, why, like a jackhammer for what would seem like forever. She wouldn't be able to escape. She knew the truth of this in her bones because every night when she got home, something would trigger her nephew's curiosity, and the whys would pop out of Will's mouth like mushrooms after a rain. No answer was ever enough to stop the flood of questions, only Kate's temper. But she was at work now, so the luxury of anger was unavailable. She took a deep breath and tried to exhale her frustrations. It didn't help that the girl wore a frilly yellow dress more appropriate for church than walking garden paths. Kate despised church clothes. Well, not the clothes really, it wasn't their fault. It was more that anyone who wore them reminded her of the early tyranny of her crazy mother and her crazy mother's church.

"Because they grow and mess up the shape they are designed to have," she answered when it became clear that the girl was still waiting for an answer to her question. Planning to bore the child and make her go away, Kate launched into a history lesson. "You see the grounds of this place were created in the style of a classic French garden, where everything is lush and beautiful, but orderly. The

French like to trim their trees and shrubs to mimic certain shapes, so we do that here, too. Sometimes it's a square, sometimes a circle, sometimes a cone. We even have animal-shaped bushes past that wall." She pointed behind the girl. "The French kings used to use their gardens as a deterrent to their enemies. They would invite kings from other countries to their castles and take them for a walk in the gardens, showing them that if they could dominate nature like this, they could surely dominate the other king's army. Their gardens were supposed to inspire fear and awe, yet also be beautiful."

She paused briefly, but the girl didn't interrupt.

"So anyway, you see how that row of trees all have their branches cut into a box shape?" Kate pointed to the neighboring row she had finished yesterday. "See how the tree I'm working on kind of looks like the ones in that row on the top part but the sides of it are more scraggly?"

The blond curls nodded twice.

"Well, nature doesn't like straight lines and branches grow willy nilly all over the place poking out of the box." She waved her arms around and wagged her tongue and crossing her eyes for good measure, not that the child could likely see such detail that far down. Kate had been working at the very top of the tree, about three stories in the air. The scissors lift was at its full height and therefore less stable, so her performance made it wobble a bit.

The girl laughed.

"My job is to cut the branches off where they extend beyond that box."

"I don't see a box," the girl said matter-of-factly.

"It's an imaginary box."

"Oh. That's probably why the branches won't stay inside of it. They can't imagine it."

"Right, I guess." Kate studied her for a few seconds and figured her to be about seven or eight. Interesting mind for a child that young, she thought. Kate was done, though. The two minute effort at entertainment exhausted her. She rotated the bill of her cap forward to block the sun and picked up her trimmer.

"Shouldn't someone be watching you? Don't you have a family you need to go to?" Kate wanted to get back to work. She could leave for the day when this row was finished.

"Yes, but they are inside that building over there." The child pointed to the head groundskeeper's cottage. "I'd rather be outside."

So she was on an adventure, sneaking out from parental supervision. Kate usually rooted for the escapee, but she just couldn't have the girl around. She didn't rope the area off before she started working and could get written up for that if the groundskeeper came looking for the girl and saw Kate's lapse. She needed this job. It was perfect; she got to be outside and alone. The work didn't involve complex decisions, yet was always new. Seeing the trees in this way, up close, where they didn't even look like trees anymore had also changed her painting, her real work, for the better.

"Look, it's not safe near the lift, and I can't work with you down there. Plus it's really loud if you don't have ear protection once I start this thing back up." She pointed to the trimmer. "What if a branch hits you or I drop a tool?" Kate was piling up the reasons like bricks in a wall to keep the girl out. "I'd feel awful, you'd be hurt, and your parents would be angry. I'd get in trouble too," she added, playing to the sense of guilt most children have about getting someone else in trouble.

"I have five brothers and sisters. They won't miss me. Dad says he can barely count us all."

Ouch, Kate thought.

"Can I sit on that bench over there out of the way and watch you?" The child pointed to a wooden bench that had always looked odd to Kate. All the other benches were stone and arranged in groupings close to the paths. This was just an ugly, utilitarian bench, illogically located in the corner between two buildings about fifty yards away. You even had to walk on the grass to get to it, which was strongly discouraged with small wooden signs sprinkled liberally through the gardens.

"Um, okay." Kate couldn't think of a reason to tell her no. If the child was out of danger and not talking to her, that was fine by her. Shepherding children was not part of the job description.

The girl walked over to the bench, sat down and scrunched herself to the back for support, which made her legs stick straight out. Maybe she was younger than Kate thought.

"Hey, how old are you?" Kate had to yell.

"Seven," the girl yelled back and held up seven fingers, all five of her right hand and the thumb and pinkie of her left.

Got the age right at least Kate said to herself, savoring the little victory as she turned back to her tree. It was strange, though, that the girl didn't offer any extra information. Most kids did when you asked them their age. I like ponies, they volunteer. I'm in second grade, they say. My brother is four, and so on ad nauseum.

Almost an hour later, after she had worked her way down the tree, she looked over to the bench, and the girl was still there, just watching. It was about time for lunch, so Kate pushed the lever to lower the lift all the way to the ground and then drove it to the next tree, parking it there. She got her lunch from the cooler she had stashed a few yards away in the shade of the next row of trees. She'd have to work on those tomorrow. After taking a long drink of water from the jug inside, Kate walked her sandwiches and soda over to the bench.

"Are you hungry?" Kate said, still standing facing the girl, casting a shadow over her. Kate was happy to share; she wasn't terribly excited about lunch since it was the end of the month and peanut butter and jelly was the family's lot for the next three days.

"No, but I don't mind if you eat your lunch here with me."

Kate laughed, more of a snort really. "Thanks. Very generous of you. I think I don't mind if I do." She sat down on the shady side of the bench and peeled the foil back from her first sandwich. How the noon sun wasn't melting the little girl in her tights and that dress with all its layers was beyond her.

"What's your name?" Kate asked.

"Isabella. What's yours?"

"That's a lovely name. I'm Kate."

"Pleased to meet you," Isabella said.

"Ditto. You have nice manners, Isabella."

"Thank you. You do too."

Kate laughed. "Not really. You're just bringing out the best in me. Are you in school?"

"Yes."

"What grade?"

"Second."

Kate ate for a while.

"So why is your family visiting Mr. Barry?"

"He's my father's brother. I think they are fighting about something."

"With all you kids around? That's not cool." While Kate didn't like children much, it was parents who bore the brunt of her hatred. Most didn't even like their children, as far as she could tell. And she knew firsthand what really bad ones could do. When she would rant about her dislike of parents and children in bars with her friends in New York, someone would eventually remind her that without a person wanting to be her parent she would never have been born. "That would have been fine," she would answer. "I didn't ask for this." And she meant it, although her friends never believed her. Thankfully, no one was mean enough to say if it was that bad, why didn't she kill herself. Because then she would have to say that she had tried. Three times. But not lately.

They sat in silence, Kate's chewing the only sound. The artist in Kate wondered how the two of them looked from a distance on that hidden bench. A tall, rangy woman in dirty denim overalls and a slightly less dirty black t-shirt wearing a red cap hiding short, straight brown hair, a few leaves sticking to her, and a blue-eyed blonde girl less than half the woman's size in a yellow crinoline dress, white tights and black shoes with a bow in her waist-length, curly hair. The sun hit the girl like a spotlight, and Kate was in the shadow. The border couldn't have been clearer or more appropriate if Kate had painted it herself. And she would paint that scene one day, from the perspective of the lift she decided. She closed her eyes to burn the image into her brain and cursed herself for not bringing her digital camera. The burning and the cursing done, she changed her focus to the work she had done today. She always had been good at shifting gears. Too good sometimes.

She felt proud as she gazed at the trees and saw that the lines and planes of the intended design were reappearing. As she sat, her own feet easily touching the ground, she turned to look at the girl, who responded with a smile and then returned her own gaze to the trees.

"Do you like the way the trees look?" Kate asked.

"I do, very much," Isabella said.

More silence, which Kate normally loved, but which seemed lonely now somehow.

"Did you come here from church?"

"No. It's not Sunday." Isabella looked at Kate and frowned slightly in confusion.

Well that explained why the gardens were so quiet. It was Monday. It was always quiet on summer Mondays – no school groups.

"I guess time gets away from me sometimes. So, if not church, why are you so dressed up?"

"We were in court."

"Oh crap. I'm sorry. What for?" Kate had personal experience with courtrooms, and she knew they were no place for a child. Or anyone without money or power. But most places are like that.

"My mommy's mommy wants me to live with her."

"Just you?" Kate asked, thinking of the brothers and sisters. Isabella nodded.

"Where do you want to live?"

"That's what the judge asked me. I don't know. I wish I could live here, in the trees. They could scare off the bad guys."

She hopped down from the bench. "I better go. Thanks for teaching me about the French trees. Bye." Then she left, turning once to wave, with a large sweep like she used before, and headed to the cottage.

The black shoes carefully carried the yellow dress toward the cottage. Isabella had to leap from stone to stone because they were spaced for an adult's stride. She was pretty athletic and managed the leaps with some grace. Kate enjoyed watching her effort. But before she got to the cottage, a man came racing out and grabbed her hand, jerking her feet off the ground. He carried her that way back into the cottage, shaking her and yelling. Almost immediately after the door closed it opened again, and the cottage disgorged the man and a woman and five other kids. Isabella followed a few feet behind holding her left arm. They all got into a van; it coughed to life and drove away, the tires spitting gravel.

Kate fought a stupid urge to run after the van. What could she do anyway? Get the license plate number? Was it actually abuse? Maybe, she thought. Was it her business? Definitely not. She sat there for longer than she intended to, stewing in the toxic soup of caring and helplessness. She got back on the lift, sad and angry, and pushed the lever hard. The sudden upward thrust caused her to lose her balance and nearly fall. She hit the stop button in a panic and nearly fell off a second time. That was close, she realized. Focus on your work, she told herself, not on someone else's problems.

Starting over, she raised herself slowly back to her stopping place. The sun had moved so she didn't need her cap to shade her eyes or her neck. She tossed it to the ground, and it floated down, momentarily caught on a breeze Kate couldn't feel. She was still unsettled two trees later when she finished the row. Should I have said something or done something, she wondered? No, it probably would have made it worse for the girl later. She decided to take a rare walk around the garden before she went home to calm down and enjoy the parts she didn't work on: the flowers, the lawns that were soft as a puppy's ear, and the fish ponds with their singing frogs.

"Bye, Kate. Have a good night."

Oscar's greeting startled her out of her thoughts. He drove the truck that picked up the worker's trimmings at the end of the day. He'd been working on the topiaries and he was heading over to the sycamores to collect her branch piles.

"Yeah, thanks. You, too." She didn't know Oscar very well, but she liked him. It was easier in her world to like people she didn't know well. They didn't usually cross paths since he worked the second shift, but she thought he was some sort of artist too. Seeing him, though, meant she was running late, not that it really mattered. She lived with her sister and her sister's kids and didn't have any responsibilities other than making a financial contribution to rent and expenses and mowing the yard every now and then. It being August in South Carolina, the yard was dormant. Kate locked up the lift and grabbed her cap, then collected her cooler and strapped it to the back of her bike for the ride to her sister's house.

Eighteen years ago their parents divorced, and Kate went to live with their father while Ellie stayed with their mother. It was a horrible split, months of fighting and accusations. And court. He should have taken them both, and he was willing to, but their mother's lawyer argued for a split of the children, like they were furniture or a business, and won. Ellie tried to make the best of it, accepting their mother's religion, going to church daily as required and separating herself from all they had shared as sisters. Kate loved being with their father until he died in a car accident when Kate was 17, the summer before she went to college. Years later, when Ellie left the church, the sisters slowly started to re-connect.

The rental house she now shared with Ellie didn't feel like home, even though Kate had lived there two years. But it would do for now; the arrangement allowed her to paint and draw and gather her strength for another stint in New York. She preferred living alone, but Ellie didn't demand much of her. The house was old and in need of some structural work, but Ellie kept it clean and neat, inside and out. When they moved in, she painted it a paler version of dandelion yellow, which made it quite cheery. Yellow is a tricky color, Kate had cautioned her, but it was easy to see that Ellie picked a good shade.

Ellie claimed she married Ray to get away, but Kate liked to remind her that a bus could have done the same with les pain. They divorced two years ago and should have done the deed sooner. Ray had been paying child support regularly, but with the economy, payments were sporadic now. Ellie's skills as a seamstress kept her busy with steady work she could do at home. So she and Kate were each saving a little and planning for separate futures. It was still a tough arrangement. They were so different, it was often hard for Kate to believe they were related.

Kate turned off the road and coasted down the long gravel driveway to the house, avoiding the potholes which liked to bounce the cooler off her bike. It was already held together with bungie cords because the seal was busted from one too many falls. Kate pulled around the back of Ellie's house, parked her bike and unhooked the cooler. Then she noticed the flies. And the dog's body next to the swing set. Oh no, poor Cody. He was old, though, and Kate figured that one too many games of Frisbee had worn his heart out. Kate consoled herself with the fact he had had a great life. She wondered if Ellie knew yet.

"You're home," Ellie announced through the open kitchen window. She had her hair in a bandana which made her look like a young, white Aunt Jemimah. It suited her, like motherhood suited her.

"What happened to Cody? Did he just keel over?" Kate walked over to the dog, knelt down, and answered her own question. He had been shot twice. Once in the chest and once in the leg. She cradled the old lab's head and stroked his fur and looked coldly at Ellie. "Who did this?"

"Ray came by. He wanted to stop paying child support. He had been drinking, and he was really angry. He tried to take the kids, he said he could take care of them for less than it was costing him to pay me. I yelled at him to stop, and Cody attacked him. So he shot him. Will was right next to him. I just got him inside now. He won't let me bury Cody. I don't know what to do." Ellie started to cry, but she had no tears left. It was awful to see. Ellie was thin and small already, but the horror had depleted her, sucked her dry.

"The fucking bastard. I'll kill him. When did it happen?"

"Only an hour ago."

Shit, Kate thought. If only she hadn't been strolling around the garden thinking about some stranger's kid. "Where did he go?"

"I don't know. I called the police. They said shooting a dog wasn't a crime."

"But attempted kidnapping is. Did you know he owned a gun?"

"They won't do anything, Kate. Ray's family has a lot of friends, remember?"

"I will, then."

"No, it will be okay. I don't think he'll come back."

"How can you know that? And anyway, he killed Cody."

"I just do. This was the end for him. I think he shocked himself. He isn't that bad a man. He's just. . . He left the gun." Ellie pulled it out of her pocket and held it up. It was a .38, Kate realized, a pretty gun.

"Let me have it," Kate walked up to the window.

"No. I'm keeping it."

"No, you're not. Not with kids in the house. Give it to me."

Ellie handed it through the torn screen. "What are you going to do?"

"Throw it away. Then we need to move so he can't find us."

"We're an 'us' now?" Ellie said, smiling through her misery.

136

"I guess so."

Kate took Emily's car and drove toward the river. She was going to throw the gun in the deepest part just past the bridge on the outskirts of town, but then she saw Ray's car at the 7-11. It was easy to recognize, a dark green El Camino. She pulled in next to it. He wasn't in the car, so she got out to look inside the store. Not there either. She felt the gun in the pocket of her overalls as she looked around the back. She checked the bathrooms. Locked. She waited until both occupants left - neither of them Ray - before she got back in her car. She didn't know what to do, so she waited.

Thirty minutes later, she saw him walking across the road towards his car.

"Ray," she called.

"Yo bitch. What the fuck do you want?"

He was wasted. Kate didn't think he recognized her, cursing was just how he addressed women.

Kate raised the gun to shoot him, but he fell down in the street before she could pull the trigger. She walked over to him.

"I hurt my ankle. Help me up."

She did, and he stumbled the rest of the way across the street to his car. He still didn't recognize her, so he wasn't suspicious when she went to her car and got a towel and pressed it against his head.

"You're bleeding."

"So?"

She pressed the nose of the gun into the towel and was surprised at how easy it was to pull the trigger. Ray slumped over and she got back in her car. The parking lot was deserted and no one was behind the counter at the 7-11. No one had seen anything.

It was after 9:30pm when Kate got home and still not quite dark. Ellie was in the backyard digging a hole for Cody. Kate snuck inside and washed the blood off her hands, then she went upstairs to Will's room. She would figure out what to do with the towel later, after they moved. Will was sitting at the window, watching his mother bury his dog in the backyard.

"Come outside with me, okay?" Will said.

"Sure," Kate answered.

"I need to get a jar first. I want to look for ants. I want to find the ones that bite and put them in my daddy's bed so they bite him and he dies." He looked at Kate defiantly, knowing he had said something Ellie would correct him for. He was testing her.

"I don't blame you."

"You don't?"

"No. But you can't go through with it. You can think about it, but you can't do it. Okay?"

"Okay."

Will dug in the dirt looking for ants but found only worms. Pete woke up and started crying so Ellie went in to get him. She came outside holding the baby, and they all watched Will dig. Kate noticed how the porch light made his light brown hair gleam, giving it a little halo.

"I got some beer while I was out," Kate said. "It's in the fridge."

"Thank god," Ellie said, wiping Pete's nose. "I could use a beer."

TOO CLOSE FOR COMFORT

"That was a super fun race," Allison said to Jim as they pedaled side by side up the hill leading out of the park. "Perfect weather, a good venue and clean water. And the bagels weren't stale."

"You don't ask for much," Jim said, laughing.

"I like a fresh bagel. And I was really afraid there were going to be too many people. I think they were at capacity, but it didn't feel crowded." Allison hadn't fastened her helmet strap, and without its anchor the bright blue helmet was sitting askew on her mass of blonde hair, making her look drunk or deranged.

"You're right. It did work out well, didn't it? There were a lot of people, but not a lot of jerks. And they spaced out the start waves well. I felt like a kid again, just swimming and biking and running for the joy of it. That's how it's supposed to be. And it never hurts to walk away with a couple of awards. I'm whacked now, though." As if to prove his claim, Jim barely dodged a couple of slower moving racers and almost spilled his pack. "Wobbly legs," he called ahead to Allison who had navigated better, and grinned.

"Yeah, I'm not sure I'm fully functional yet either," she said when he caught back up. "So can you drive home with wobbly legs?" she asked. "I know we had a deal, but I see a big nap in my future, and I don't want it to start when I'm behind the wheel."

"No problem. You did great. You deserve a nap."

They had to park for the race in the overflow lot, almost a mile away, so they rode their bikes only until the pavement turned to the type of rough gravel that is the sworn enemy of thin bicycle tires. Jim smiled at his wife as they stopped to dismount.

"You know, we should put this one on the calendar for next year."

"Definitely. We could even make a weekend of it and camp the night before," Allison said, pushing her bike with her hand on the back of the seat.

They walked companionably past other clusters of happy and tired athletes. It was nice to be around happy people, Allison thought. Even if some were just happy the race was over, everyone was happier than when the day started. It was their communal contribution to the happiness of the world, she thought.

"Hey, should we get some pansies on the way home?" Allison was eager to plant something in the new raised beds Jim built in the spring. Getting the race over with meant they could focus on the house and the yard; that's what Jim promised.

"Sure. You want to go to the Ivy Nursery? It's on the way. Maybe we could get a houseplant or two to fill up some of the empty space."

They had recently bought a house after years of tiny apartments, and their furniture and art underwhelmed the space. It made Jim feel unsettled.

"If we can remember which ones are not toxic to animals. I don't want to come home to poisoned cats one day." Allison mimed dead – eyes closed, head back, tongue out, arms extended, wrists bent.

"Neither do I," Jim had to agree, shaking his head at the performance.

"Ah, you hate the cats."

"Not all the time," Jim pleaded. "Only when they sleep on my head. But now Gracie never does anything wrong."

"You're right about that." Allison loved Jim's dog, a sleek retired racing greyhound faster than the two of them put together, but the cats were hers and dated back to her life before Jim. She would always stick up for them.

"I bet someone at the nursery has a list or a book that can tell us what's safe."

"That's probably true. Ugh, I've got the chills all of a sudden for some reason." Allison stopped and Jim held her bike as she pulled her sweatshirt out of her bag and struggled it on over her helmet. She was too tired to take the helmet off and find a place for it in her bag.

"Your body temperature is dropping back to normal after the effort of the race and normal feels cold now. It's temporary; you'll be fine in a few minutes in this sun." Despite his reassuring words, Allison knew Jim would keep an eye on her; it was a side effect of being married to an ER doctor. Kind of a nice one too, she thought. She liked being cared for.

They were almost back at their truck when they heard it. A dog was barking itself into a frenzy somewhere. It sounded muffled, as if the noise came from inside a building, but there were no houses around. It also sounded strangely tired, as if it didn't really want to bark anymore or it had been barking for a long time. The noise got louder as they approached their truck, and then they saw the dog in the driver's seat of a dusty black Honda on their right.

"Can you believe that dog has been locked in that car since we unloaded this morning?" said a woman lifting her bicycle into the truck next to the dog's car.

That stopped them dead.

"What?" Jim said. "Are you serious? That asshole." He looked at his watch and at the sun. It was almost 1pm.

With a jerk of her head to the side, Allison shed her bike helmet then grabbed a water bottle from the cage on her bike. She thrust the bike at Jim and ran over to try and dribble water to the dog through a crack in the rear window.

"Will it take any?" asked Jim.

"No, and I'm getting the back seat all wet trying, but I don't care. Who leaves their dog in a car while they do a race? That's like four or five hours it has to stay here with all the commotion around. It's horrible and cruel. The fucking bastard."

Allison was as worked up as Jim had ever seen her.

"It's stopped barking," Jim said hopefully, trapped holding the two bikes in the middle of the road.

"I think it's a she, and she's stopped barking because she's terrified. She's crawled under the steering wheel, in the well by the pedals. Poor thing. She's just looking at me like she's begging for me to help her."

"But she won't drink?"

"No. And oh geez. She's peed on the driver's seat."

"The guy deserves it. She must have been here since way before eight."

"Totally in the sun, too." Allison squinted at the sky. "And with all that long black fur. This isn't right. This isn't legal is it?"

"I don't know. Hold on. Let me roll the bikes to the truck." Jim covered the last few yards at a trot even with the meandering bikes and leaned them against the truck, dumping his backpack on the ground.

"I'm calling 911," she announced as he returned, still in his helmet.

"Hold on. Do you think we should? I mean the dog is clearly miserable but not in clinical distress. It's not an emergency, and I'm not sure it's illegal. She gets some shade from the dashboard down in the well, too." Jim was peering into the car from the other side and bumped his helmet on the window which made the dog bark, but she didn't move from her spot.

"She's not even panting, just salivating when she barks which makes her look kind of scary."

"So she's not worth helping because of how she looks?" Allison was furious.

"Did you try the door?" Jim ignored her comment.

"Yeah," Allison answered, pulling on the locked handle of the driver's side and all the other doors again for good measure. "I'm calling." She ran to their truck to get her cell phone.

Jim followed her. "Whoa. Think about it. Let's not overreact. It's probably only 75 degrees now, and it was cool this morning. The race is over except for the stragglers. I bet the guy will be back soon." He went back to the car and put his hand on the roof. "The metal doesn't feel raging hot either. Maybe people walking by bother her more than the sun."

"Yeah, and then what will the dog's life be like when the guy does get back? We have an obligation. How could we walk away?" Allison ignored Jim's report about the car's roof. She wanted to do something, needed to. "He'll probably beat her for peeing on his seat, which you know she wouldn't have done if she were okay."

"You don't know that."

"I don't, but it's not a risk I'm willing to take. I feel responsible."

"Fine. Call." Jim stalked back to the truck and took the front wheel off his bike and put the frame in the back. He slid the wheel in and tied wheel and frame down. "I feel sorry for the guy," he called back to her.

"What? Why? You'd never do something like this." Allison had turned her phone on and was halfway to the Honda, but hadn't dialed the magic numbers. Maybe Jim was right. Or maybe I'm afraid of being wrong, she thought. She was mad at Jim for muddying the waters. Allison noticed the woman who reported on the dog had finished packing up and was waving as she drove off. She hated her too all of a sudden. Why hadn't the woman done something? Why did she always have to pick up other people's slack?

"No, I wouldn't," Jim answered. "But I have you, and we have neighbors and a life filled with friends we can count on and a kennel we like and a dog sitter. That guy is probably all alone and has no other options. Maybe he doesn't have enough money to hire someone to let his dog out. Maybe his wife left him."

"So? Then he shouldn't have a dog and most certainly shouldn't be wasting money on a triathlon entry fee. God, how can you not see how bad this is? Why are we fighting? You were upset too. Now, you care more about the guy than the innocent dog?"

"No, but why do you need to be right? Why can't my view of the situation be right sometime?" Jim picked up and skipped a rock on the flat road in frustration.

"Because yours would let this dog die, or at least have a rotten life."

"The dog is not dying at the moment, and why is its life more important than ours?"

"What a ridiculous thing to say!" Allison wheeled around.

"Well, is it? You didn't answer me. I think everything will be fine, and you want to make a big deal out of it. Yeah, it looked bad at first, and we would never leave Gracie in the car like that. I grant you it's an unpleasant thing to see, but everyone shouldn't have to follow our rules. It isn't that hot, the dog clearly isn't in physical distress, and you're taking that woman's word for it that the dog has been in the car for hours. People live differently. Who are we to judge?" Jim thrust his chin at the space where the woman was. "And why didn't she do something instead of passing it on to us? I just don't want to make the wrong choice. I don't want to be the judgmental jerk."

"So doing nothing is better than doing something and risking being wrong? That's crazy. You are a coward. And why would those women lie anyway?"

"They probably wouldn't, but you don't know everything, that's my only point. And I am not a coward, I'm just trying to be reasonable. Look, we're tired and hungry and maybe not thinking clearly," Jim's voiced and energy trailed off.

"I'm thinking clearly enough."

Allison started dialing. Jim gave up and worked on getting her bike and the rest of the gear into the truck. Jim heard Allison reporting the situation to the emergency operator, exaggerating just enough to be annoying. So he was a coward and she was a liar. What a pair. Jim took his helmet off and rubbed his head and sat on the only patch of grass he could find.

"What'd they say?"

"They will notify animal control. That's all I wanted. Hopefully they will get here in time, and he'll be scared into treating that dog better." Allison figured that this would be the end of their fight, that Jim would apologize.

"Maybe. Are you ready?" Jim said in a flat voice.

"Yeah, almost." Allison looked around to see if there was anything else she could do, anyone else she could appeal to.

"We should probably get going. We're at the far end of the lot, and I don't want a confrontation with this guy."

"Are you afraid of that jerk?"

"Yeah, aren't you?" I thought you decided he was a bad guy who would beat his dog. I don't think he'd have a problem dealing with us hanging around his car."

"I thought you figured him for a good guy who had just run out of options this one time."

"Whatever. Don't throw my words in my face. I just don't want to meet him."

Allison looked at Jim for a few seconds, her head cocked as if she were trying to place a sound. "Fine. Let me just leave a note too." Allison rummaged in the glove compartment looking for a pen and something to write on. She found a pencil from their miniature golf outing and a grocery receipt.

"Great, you just can't leave it alone. And that receipt better not have our credit card number on it."

"It doesn't. And why should I leave it alone? I'm trying to help a poor, defenseless animal. Why are you attacking me for that?"

"I don't know. I'm just uncomfortable all of a sudden."

Allison stared at him. "Me doing the right thing makes you uncomfortable?"

"Fine. I'm an asshole. Me and the guy who locked the dog in his car and every other coward. We're all assholes."

"Don't be like that. I never called you an asshole, and I don't really think you're a coward. I just disagree with you. Don't you understand?"

"No. You know, you only see the whole world through your eyes."

"Doesn't everybody?" Allison interrupted, defiant.

"Yeah, but just not so clearly as you, I guess."

"I feel sorry for them then."

"And me," Jim whispered under his breath.

Allison glared at him.

"I'm sorry." Jim said and felt a headache coming on. You're right. Let's go home."

Allison scribbled her note and stuck it under the driver's side windshield wiper. The dog watched her but didn't bark. "I'm so worried about that dog," she said, glancing back before she got in the truck.

Jim flipped on the air conditioning and cracked the windows to help circulate the air. They joined the long line of cars, each with a bike or two strapped to the roof or trunk, creeping toward the main road. They looked like a parade of some rare breed of insect.

"If we back up, we could go out the other way," Allison turned around and saw no one was behind them yet.

"I don't know how to get home that way," Jim said.

MIGRATION

"Babe, really? You set the alarm? We're not working lunch today, remember?"

Still mostly asleep, Michael rolled onto Alma's side of the bed and onto Alma to fumble for the off button. The buzzing could not stop soon enough for him. Exhausted by his successful effort, he rolled back to his side and curled into a ball with a grunt. Michael did not like mornings.

The alarm clock was on Alma's side of the bed because Michael slept next to the wall. His apartment was small like all apartments in the city, but the bedroom was ridiculously tiny. He could stand on the bed and stick his arms out and almost touch each wall. She slept on the side with barely enough room for a bedside table because she liked to read and needed a lamp. Of course they could have gotten one of those clip-on lamps and stuck it on the headboard, but the idea of sleeping next to the wall made her feel trapped and anxious. Michael didn't mind the wall. He didn't mind much of anything, except the alarm.

Alma had been awake for over an hour, but she wasn't in a hurry to get up. And she loved the sensation of Michael's body travelling over hers. It was all she had to look forward to this morning. There was something elemental yet gentle about the way he moved, like some ancient, meandering river. He washed away her fear and rounded out the sharp edges of her life with his smallest gestures. He made living so far from home bearable and often wonderful, she thought with a twinge of guilt.

"I'm sorry," she whispered. "Remember I said I would go with Heather to her appointment?"

Michael wrestled with the covers and buried his face in the pillow. A muffled "I forgot" came from his side of the bed. Then he lifted his head. "What time is it?"

"7:30."

"Ugh. I hate Heather."

Alma laughed because Michael didn't hate anybody. She met him a little over a year ago when he caught her watching him work in the kitchen. She had been waiting tables at Bijoux for a week and he was the head chef. On that day, he was filling in on the line because they were short a cook.

"Am I doing it wrong?" he asked with a white toothed grin.

"What? No, I am sorry. I just..."

She stopped talking and he stopped chopping and looked at her and smiled.

"You know food. I can tell. I like that," he said.

"How can you tell?"

"First, you look at the plates before you take them out. And not just to see if we got the order right. It's like you're sending a child off on an adventure and hoping for the best. Second, I've seen you eat at the staff meals. You let the food teach you. I like that."

Alma didn't know what to say. Her mouth went dry as all her body's juices sped south. She was rooted to the spot but afraid her legs wouldn't hold her up another second. She had never felt such physical desire before. She had noticed on her first day that Michael was handsome, but she didn't know he could see into her, didn't know he wanted to.

Then one of the sous chefs nearly cut off his finger, and his scream broke their spell and snapped everyone to attention. Michael ran to him and grabbed his hand, tied a kitchen towel around the finger and thrust his hand above his head.

"Sit," he commanded, and pointed to the step ladder near the freezer.

"Can you drive?" he asked Alma.

"Yes," she said, although she hadn't driven yet in America.

"Take him to the hospital. My car is out back. It's yellow." He fished in his pocket. "Here are the keys."

Somehow Alma and Steve, she learned his name on the ride, made it to the hospital without further injury from either impatient cabbies or crazed bike messengers, the two biggest hazards in the city. He got stitched up as Alma waited and worried. They didn't get back until after the dinner rush was over. Alma was disappointed about losing a night of tips, but realized there was nothing she could do about it now. It seemed a small price to pay for being a good employee and getting to drive a car in New York for the first time.

When they walked back into the kitchen and Alma saw Michael cleaning up, her feelings threatened to overwhelm her again. But everyone started teasing Steve, so that provided a good distraction. He took most of it good naturedly.

"You have a nice car," Alma said to Michael when she finally handed the keys back to him.

"Thanks. I bought it when I turned sixteen. My dad loved to work on cars, and he had a thing for Chevys, so we nurtured it back from the grave. They're not many of those old clunkers still around."

"It is much prettier than a clunker," Alma said, surprised at her boldness. In the past, she would have found a reason to leave by now.

"Ah, well, she still needs more work. I just can't afford to do it. Thanks though. And thanks for taking Steve. You were just right there and, well, I figured I would get to talk to you when you came back."

Alma blushed.

Michael wiped his hands on his apron and suck out the right one. "I'm Michael."

"I'm Alma."

"Hey lovebirds and everyone else! We still got guests and they may want desert and we may want to bring it to them, right? To, I don't know, make some money and pay all you losers? Jesus effing Christ! Get to work!"

Alma's eyes widened, and Michael laughed.

"You're not afraid of Nick are you? Come on, he's all bluster. You can't go out there anyway; you have blood all over you."

Alma untied her apron which had caught the largest splotch and put it in the hamper.

"Can she help with the dishes, oh great chef?" Nick asked.

"Of course I will," Alma said and hurried off. She didn't want to be noticed by management for anything other than hard work. She didn't want to get in trouble.

Thanks to scheduling conflicts, it was two weeks before they had their first date. In between, Alma spent a lot of time studying Michael in the kitchen of the small restaurant where they worked. She wasn't sure why he liked her so much, but she could tell he did. There were far prettier girls in the restaurant and all over the city. He would later explain when she asked that it was because she was so self-contained, that she seemed to carry a whole world within her. She laughed because at the time she was so homesick, so in a way he was right. He also said he liked her hair, the way it looked like a golden version of the Spanish moss that graced the trees where he grew up. He said he would take her to South Carolina one day.

For that first date he packed a picnic lunch and they rode the Staten Island ferry. Michael was horrified that she hadn't done any of the classic New York touristy things yet. It ended up being a miserable day, rainy and windy, but the ferry was empty and Alma loved being away from the city. They had been spending most nights together since then, usually at his place when they had to work because his apartment was closer to the restaurant. They spent their days off at her place.

It wasn't the life she expected when she came to New York. A fire at her family's restaurant in Turkey forced them to close for repairs. At the same time, her aunt in New York had just had a baby with Down's syndrome, and she needed help desperately. It was so sad; her husband had left her and she wasn't well herself. Since there was no work at the restaurant and Alma was the only one with a passport thanks to an old school trip, she volunteered to go. It was harder work than she thought, but her aunt was so grateful. Then the baby died, and her aunt went back to Turkey. By that time Alma had met Michael. So she kept the apartment which was in a building where illegal immigrants weren't bothered and felt herself starting to split in two, the homesickness sharing space with the good things she was discovering in New York.

Now she was afraid to go home, even though she missed her mother and father and brothers and sisters and the whole mess of her extended family. She was afraid she was too different for her old life, afraid that she couldn't go back. She grieved for the loss of something that still existed.

She was able to send home money and she knew she was lucky. And she loved Michael, but their relationship confused her. He was American, with the accent to prove it, but in private he seemed more like an immigrant, like her. He said it was because he was black. "When your great-great-great grandpa comes over on a slave ship, you never quite fit in," he would say when she questioned him. But he could fake it when he needed to, a skill he thought she should learn. "You are too honest," he would tell her. "America is about projecting an image. You need to act, to build up a shield or you'll never get what you want."

"You're my shield," she would tell him. And he was. She felt completely different when she was with him. Sometimes, if she let it, this new life felt better than home. But it wasn't really. She knew it could end in an instant. It wasn't real. It wasn't family; it wasn't blood.

Alma pushed her thoughts aside and yawned and stretched. She rubbed her eyes and blinked the rest of her sleep away and got up to go to the bathroom. She brushed her teeth and took a shower and when she came out, dressed, but still squeezing the water from her unruly and extra absorbent hair, Michael had gotten up and made coffee.

"Do you want some toast?" he asked.

Michael was less than enthusiastic about Heather and didn't approve of Alma going with her anywhere. He thought Heather had bad energy and attracted disaster, but he wasn't about to let his girlfriend leave the apartment hungry.

Heather started at the restaurant about a month ago and attached herself to Alma like a suckerfish; at least that was how Michael saw it. Alma didn't mind Heather, but she didn't really like her. She felt a sense of duty towards her because she saw helping Heather as a way to pay back her luck.

"I'll take a piece with me. I'm afraid I'm going to be late."

"Okay."

He wrapped two pieces of toast from a loaf of Russian bread that he made the day before. He wanted them to open a restaurant together and he was tinkering with bread recipes for when they were ready. It was an interesting thought, but Alma didn't let herself get too excited or frightened about the possibility.

"I need a book or magazine, too" she said, looking around the apartment. Alma hated being on the subway without something to read. Paper made one of the best shield.

"Take this. I just finished it." Michael thrust a book into her hands. They kissed, and she was out the door.

"You sure you don't want to take the car?" Michael yelled down the stairs.

He had started calling it "the car" instead of "my car" a couple of months ago.

"No, I'm good," she called back up to him.

"Okay. See you at the restaurant. Be safe. I love you."

"I will and me too. Bye." She waved over her head and jogged the rest of the stairs.

Waiting for the train, she ate the toast before she realized it was the first day of Ramadan.

"Shit," she said aloud. She knew Michael didn't do it on purpose, but she also knew he hated God. Or rather hated religion. She would have to lie to her mother and make it up somehow. He asked her why she still followed the rituals when she didn't believe, and she didn't have an answer. At least not one she could explain to him. What she knew in her heart was that they made her feel safe, the same way he was starting to.

On the train, Alma took the book out of her bag and laughed out loud. It was *The Old Man and the Sea*, a book she loved and had lent to Michael last month. He had a terrible memory. She opened the worn pages – she had bought the book secondhand – and a note slipped out.

"Will you marry me?"

Her stomach surged into her throat and her heart started racing. The blood drained from her head and she felt dizzy. She hadn't thought about marriage, not once. She thought about family all the time, but not marriage. Why, she wondered, as she fingered the note. It was written on the receipt she had used as a bookmark. He'd dated his question, so she wouldn't think it was a mistake. She knew he knew how she thought about things, where her mind went first.

She wished she had someone to talk to about it. All their friends were Michael's friends. And her family, her family would tell her to come home and be the girl who left. Maybe Heather? Ah, but not today, today would be a bad time to ask Heather for advice on marriage.

Thirty minutes, several imaginary lifetimes and one change of trains later, Alma rang the doorbell of Heather's apartment in Harlem. She buzzed Alma in immediately. As she trudged up the four flights, she could see Heather stick her head out of her apartment.

"Thanks for coming," Heather called down the staircase.

Alma looked up and shrugged. "Not a problem. Are you ready?"

"Almost. Come on in. I'm just hunting for some Tylenol. I have the worst headache. Do you want some tea? There is chamomile and yerba mate, depending on whether you want to be up or down!" Heather flounced theatrically into the bedroom. She seemed less concerned than Alma thought she should be. But Alma upbraided herself. Do not judge, she repeated for the hundredth time since Heather asked her to come. It won't help anything.

"Your hair's still wet," Heather exclaimed, picking the strands of curls off Alma's back. Heather liked to touch people.

"It takes forever to dry in this weather. Can I use your phone for a second?"

"Is it important? I don't want to be late. I'm afraid I'll chicken out."

"No. No, I guess not."

It started to rain as they walked to the subway. Heather wanted to go to a clinic in New Jersey, so they had to take the subway to Penn Station, and then a train and then a taxi. She talked the whole way and Alma for once was happy to listen because it drowned out the noise in her own head.

"Ben kept offering to come, but I just didn't want him to. I barely liked him enough to sleep with him. I can't believe the condom broke with him of all people. I mean seriously, what bad luck, right? Not that I could handle a baby even if it came from someone else's sperm. I don't think I ever want kids."

"Really? Ever?"

"Yeah. I just think they are too much trouble, that they will interfere with my plans. I mean, I don't really have my act together now, and I know it will take a long time to make it as an actress."

"Probably. But you are very good."

It was true. Alma and Michael and most of the staff at Bijoux saw Heather's last play and she was good. It was a small part, but she was believable in the strange story as an old woman who had grown a tail.

"I've got an audition tomorrow."

"That's great. What's it for?"

"It's another play, but this time a bigger part and only an off-off-Broadway instead of off-off-off Broadway!"

Alma laughed. Heather could be charming.

"So you'll be working lunches for a while?"

"Yeah, the money is crap, but it is my only option. Ben's at least paying for the abortion."

"That's nice of him."

"Yeah. He is a nice guy. I wish I liked nice guys." Heather shook her head and looked at her feet. It started to rain harder.

"Crap."

"Maybe it's sunny in New Jersey."

"Now that would be a good title for a play!" Heather said, and they both laughed.

It wasn't sunny in New Jersey, but the rain was light enough that it landed more like dandelion fuzz than water droplets on their clothes. They hailed a taxi and got to the clinic right at 10:30. As Heather paid the driver, he looked at the building and shook his head.

"What if you change your mind?"

"Excuse me?"

"What if you end up wishing you hadn't killed your baby you whore-bitch?" He drove off before Heather could answer.

"Fuck you!" she screamed at his rear bumper. "Fucking judgmental prick."

"Oh my God, that was awful of him. I am so sorry. Are you okay?" Alma asked.

"Yeah, screw him. Let's go in and get this over with."

There were fresh flowers on the receptionist's desk, but otherwise, the place looked very sad. Their seat choices consisted of hard plastic or cracking vinyl. Alma wasn't fussy, but the worn out vinyl surprised her.

"You would think an abortion clinic would be a little more sensitive about the sitting parts of a woman," she said to make Heather laugh, but Heather was now beyond laughing.

They chose the only hard plastic seats left that were next to each other.

"I feel like I should be sad or something, but I'm just nervous," Heather said.

"That's understandable. But I think they really know what they are doing."

"You're right," Heather said and smiled.

"Heather Ackerman?"

"That's me. Wow, they are punctual," Heather, looking at her watch. "I'll be back."

"Good luck. I hope it doesn't hurt."

"I kind of hope it does," Heather said.

Alma was startled, and felt for the first time that a real friendship could develop between them. Embracing pain as a part of life was something her people did well. Too well.

Alma opened her book and saw Michael's note again. She had forgotten it was there, but this time the discovery made her smile. She put the note in her pocket and started reading.

Sixteen pages later, the double doors to the procedure room burst open and a nurse ran to the receptionist. They consulted two different clipboards before the nurse called Alma's name.

"Yes, that's me. Is she ready already?" Alma asked, knowing it wasn't that simple, but not knowing what else could be happening.

"Come with me."

Alma followed the nurse into an office.

"We've called an ambulance. Your friend had a seizure of some sort. We're taking her to the hospital."

Alma heard the siren approaching.

"Do you want to ride with her, or do you have a car?"

"We came by subway and taxi. I. . ."

"You can ride in the ambulance." The nurse took her hand. "She going to get the best care. She'll be fine. Come with me.

We'll meet the ambulance out back." She smiled as best she could and got up.

When Alma got outside, the ambulance had already parked and two men opened its doors. The door of the clinic opened almost immediately and the doctor pushed Heather's bed toward the men. They lifted her in so smoothly, it was like a strange sort of ballet.

"Come on. You can ride in the back," one of them said to Alma. As she was getting in, the nurse shoved a bag at her. "Her personal items," she said.

The trip to the hospital took less than ten minutes. People were waiting for them when they arrived and the ballet was reversed. No one talked to Alma until after Heather was wheeled down a hall. Then a man with an eye patch came out from behind a desk and asked her if she could fill out some paperwork. She said she would try. All her life, Alma had hated hospitals. According to her mother, she cried from the minute she was born until the wheelchair ferrying Alma and her mother to the parking lot left the building. The she stopped. She cried again when she was in the hospital for scarlet fever and to have her tonsils out. She gathered her strength and filled out the blanks that she could and returned the paperwork and settled in to wait.

"Alma Sener?"

"Yes, that is me." Alma was dozing when she heard her name. She didn't know how much time had passed. She got up and walked over to the nurse. Her name tag was covered in stickers, but Alma could still read the name: Yvonne. "Is Heather all right?"

"No, my dear. I am afraid she passed. She didn't regain consciousness. These things sometimes happen. It must have been her time. The doctor will be out in a moment to tell you more. We'll need instructions. . ."

Alma stopped listening. She could only stare at Yvonne's feet. The feet were enclosed in the same style of clogs her mother liked for work. Alma hated those clogs.

"I have to sit down." It was a combination of the smell, and the lighting, and the sense of death hovering a foot above her head.

"Are you going to faint? Hold on sweetie. I know it must be a terrible shock. Come here."

The huge nurse set down her clipboard and wrapped her arms around Alma, nearly lifting her off her feet and took her to a chair.

"Can I get you water or a Coke?"

"No. Yes. I don't know." Alma started to cry.

"Here's a tissue." Yvonne pulled a pack from her pocket. "I'll be back with a Coke. Oh, and there's Dr. Spalding."

Alma tried to stand up, but the doctor motioned her down and sat next to her.

"Your friend had a blood clot in her brain. She felt no pain, and there was nothing we could do. The bleeding was too severe. It was a blessing she died actually before we could put her on life support. I know that may seem shocking to hear, but its true."

"It is not shocking. I understand."

They sat in silence for a minute.

"Was it from the abortion?"

"No. It was unrelated. She was a ticking time bomb. I'm sorry, that's a crude way to put it. It's just been a long day."

"It's okay. Can I use a phone?"

The doctor pulled his cell phone out of his pocket. "Here. Use mine."

"Thank you."

She called the restaurant. Michael wasn't there yet. She told them she might be late. She handed the phone back.

"That's it? You don't need to call anyone else?"

"No. Not now. I need to go home now."

"Okay." The doctor patted her arm and heaved himself out of the chair. He walked with a limp back down the hall.

Alma picked up Heather's things and left before the nurse could come back.

"Hey, you're back earlier than I thought," Michael said when she walked in an hour later. "I didn't have time to. . ."

"Yes."

"Really?" His eyes lit up.

"Yes. Really. Thank you for asking."

"God, I love it when you are formal!" He picked her up and spun her around and kissed her all over. "Hey, what's in the bag?"

THE ARCTIC SWALLOW

In the fertile backseat of Emily's car, Dan's vague doubt planted itself and blossomed into a visceral fear. It felt like someone had inflated a balloon inside his chest, leaving him hollow yet unable to take a full breath.

While fear was certainly a normal response to what he was going to do, the feeling was still foreign to Dan. For the past several months there had been little time for doubt and none for fear. From the moment Earth United decided to move forward, the sheer amount of work left him and the others with barely any time for sleep, much less cowardly second guessing. He enjoyed all the work, though, because everyone involved in the plan to destroy the Arctic Swallow was energized by their passion for the environment, a passion that had spilled over to all areas of their lives. The media called them eco-terrorists, but they saw themselves as saviors, not warriors. These new friends had become like family to Dan, and he would do anything for family.

Dan would be completely alone for this next stage, though. There would be no more collective energy buzzing around that made him feel like he could run a marathon barefoot, no more brainstorming in coffee shops in Freemont, no more parties in Capitol Hill basements, no more practice runs on the ferries, no more sneaking into libraries and offices. No more sharing dreams of a better, cleaner world. No more planning, just action, and just by him. This realization fueled Dan's fear even more; whoever was filling that balloon was making it so big that it was squeezing the air out of his lungs and the breakfast out of his stomach. He tried to fight it by focusing on why he was doing this. He was preparing to sink a cruise ship because Earth United decided it was the only way to stop the polluting, destructive, selfish tourist traffic to the Arctic. And Dan believed his leaders. This noble cause of keeping humans from destroying what was left of the pristine far north felt like what he was born for. It had to be. He'd failed at everything else he'd ever tried in his twenty-nine years. Other jobs, hobbies and friends never fit. Or they never fit for long. Something always happened, but the last failure hurt the most.

Everything had been going so well at the research station, too. He'd been on the job for about two years and was close to finishing his project. Then they lost their funding. Some said it was because of Professor McGrath's ineptitude, but Dan couldn't bring himself to believe that. He liked the professor as a person and a scientist. In fact he liked him so much that after things fell apart in Ecuador, Dan followed him to Seattle where he said he could get Dan a post at the University of Washington working in the lab. When Dan got to Seattle, though, and went to the address McGrath gave him, a woman answered the door and said she'd never heard of anyone named McGrath. Then he went to the university, and the secretary in the Marine Sciences department said the same thing. Dan called the number he'd written down before they parted at the airstrip in Ecuador over and over until someone finally answered. The someone said she was the professor's sister and that McGrath had died of a heart attack on the flight back to Seattle. Dan stayed drunk for three days. He only quit because he got the flu and was too sick to leave his apartment to get booze. Earth United's members and mission filled the empty spaces in Dan's soul. He couldn't stand being empty.

Dan was startled by the car swerving violently left then back right.

"Idiot!" Randy yelled at the biker, who was having trouble balancing his bike with what looked like groceries in the saddlebags. "If you can't go straight, stay out of the road!"

The helmet nodded, taking the abuse.

"That guy gives real cyclists a bad name," grumbled Randy. Emily remained silent in the driver's seat. "If you can't get up the hills, take a car. Jesus."

Dan was grateful for Randy's temper because it stopped the loop of thoughts in his head and punctured that balloon. He closed his bright green eyes and took back control of his body with several deep breaths. He opened his eyes and checked his watch. He'd been up since before 5:00 am, but that was usual for him. He never slept long. His watch said 9:15 am. The date in the little window was off; it said August 29th instead of the 30th. He couldn't get it set right because the button had broken off. He took a few more calming breaths, felt his heart rate slow down, and decided to get a new watch when he returned.

"So we're almost there," Emily announced brightly, flicking her eyes to the rearview mirror and smiling. She was the earth mother of Earth United, always concerned about everyone's feelings, smoothing over the rare disputes, smelling good and making tea. Dan would miss her. They just passed under the sign for the Union Street exit off of Highway 5, and were about two miles from the pier. Traffic was bad, though, and they were moving slowly.

"How are you feeling?" she asked.

"Fine. Ready and excited," Dan answered from the back seat, surprised at how different his actual voice sounded from the one in his head.

"You're lying. You must be scared." Randy turned around in the passenger's seat to look at Dan.

Dan looked back with all the confidence he could muster. "Yeah, I'm scared, but I'm good to go. You can count on me." Dan knew Randy didn't like him, but he didn't know why, and it made him sad.

"Okay, Dan. I just wanted to give you a chance to back out. We don't need you to have any doubts. This is important and dangerous work." Randy paused, and rubbed the bridge of his nose with his thumb and the knuckle of his index finger. Dan had learned to recognize the gesture as Randy's way of keeping himself from saying anything cruel. "I'm as sure as I can be that we've equipped you to survive, but there are no guarantees in the Arctic. It's easy to die there. If you think it's going to be a cake walk, this is the wrong job for you."

"I know it won't be easy." Dan slid over on the seat so he could come closer to looking Randy in the eye. "But I finally feel like I am doing something that matters. I know you think I can't care as much as you because I haven't lived there and seen the loss of habitat firsthand. But I get it. I do. I'm in love with it just like you. I am willing to kill to save it, and I am willing to die." Dan's stomach rebelled against his statement.

"All right." Randy turned around with a shrug. Dan had never gotten a chance to talk to Randy one on one during the planning stage. He didn't know if he could explain himself in the short time left, or if it mattered, but he needed to try.

"The way I see it, these tourists are like locusts. And the companies that are willing to pollute the water and destroy the land to take them where they want to go are plain evil. I saw firsthand what they did in the Galapagos, and they deserve to die." Dan spat the last words. "The argument that eco-tourism supports these wild places, whether they are snow-covered or tropical, is false. It's just another rationalization for rape, and I'm sick of it." This much was completely and passionately true for Dan, or had been for the past seven years. Acting on that truth is what made his heart race and his stomach hurt.

"They have no love for these places," he continued. "They just want to check something off their life list and get a story to tell their friends. Blow up photos to put on their walls and pretend they are artists. They leave trash, they violate rules they don't understand or don't like, and they generally act like feral children. I've seen what a plastic bag can do to a sea turtle. But it's a game for them. Whoever dies with the most exotic trips wins. Someone needs to stop it. HALO and the other arctic tourism companies have got the government and the public buying their outdated rationale for polluting these places. It's all about money, and it makes me sick."

They were at a red light, so Emily turned around. Her eyes were blazing. "You hear it all the time: I want to see it before it's gone. But they are the ones making it disappear." Emily said, twisting her red hair into knots with her right hand.

"I don't know why they can't see that." Dan said.

"You'll help them see that." Emily said.

Randy shifted in his seat. Dan had heard he was not a big fan of discussing philosophy. He called it self-indulgent. 'We all agree, let's just move on and not masturbate about it,' was his favorite saying. Action, that's what Randy was about. But Dan needed to talk about it. It made him feel solid and real.

"I think some people are starting to see, but they need help, they need us. This is like operating to get rid of the last little bit of a tumor. You have to take out some healthy flesh to make sure it's gone, but in the end, the organism will live." This is what Dan told himself last night, and it felt good to say it aloud.

Emily's face in the mirror smiled at Dan. "Trust a scientist to say it so well."

Randy sighed, unfolded and re-folded his arms. He looked at the watch on his wrist and then picked up his bag to check something. Dan looked out the window, satisfied he'd said all he had in him. They were almost there anyway.

"That's a pretty speech, but this is not a time for high mindedness or pretty anything. This is work we have to do, but it is ugly and sad. Just do it right." Randy punctuated his command with a jerk of his chin and closed the subject.

Emily looked pained. "Don't mind him," she said to Dan. "I think he's nervous for you and for us." She glared at Randy's profile, and turned back to Dan. "You'll be fine if you avoid making any friends or mingling too much. Don't be a loner, they'll notice that and try to draw you out, but don't connect with anyone either. It will just make it harder. Trust me."

Dan wondered, as he had ever since he met her, what Emily's history was.

"No problem," he said.

They made the last turn onto Alaskan Way, and Emily found a place to park the car a few blocks past Pier 69. Dan opened the door and grabbed his two bags from the backseat and one from the trunk and saluted to lighten the mood.

Randy returned the salute with a flourish and smiled. That smile was like a gift; it made everything better for Dan.

"We'll send you the occasional fax with weather reports and any new instructions we may have. Are you comfortable with the code?" Randy asked.

"Absolutely," Dan responded. He was always good with numbers and puzzles.

"Then good luck and God speed," said Randy. "The world will be a different and better place when you get back."

Emily got out of the car and gave Dan a hug. She and Randy waved as she drove off, glancing once in the rear view mirror. Dan waved for a second, then made himself turn toward the ship.

"Now we just wait," Randy said.

"Do you think he'll make it?" Emily asked.

"I think he'll go through with the plan. I'm sure of it actually. That's why we picked him. But do I think he'll survive? No. His survival is not important anyway."

At the stoplight, Emily put on her signal to turn right and looked in the rear view mirror for the last time.

As Dan walked north along the wide sidewalk to Pier 69, he squinted against the power of the rare Seattle sun. He could clearly see the Arctic Swallow, and he thought how dark and imposing she looked. In fact, he realized, she looked less like a ship and more like a floating building. There was none of the bland cruise ship uniformity to her appearance. She had been built for business, not beauty. He stopped to get a good look at her. Like all icebreakers, she was tall and narrow which was good for icebreaking but bad for handling rough water. Her hull barely seemed wide enough to support the blocky tower that was the bulk of her. Most icebreakers wouldn't take the route the Arctic Swallow was planning this late in the year because of all the open water and the potential for fall storms. They were going across the Gulf of Alaska, down around the Aleutian Islands, through the Bering Strait and up to Barrow where the passengers would disembark for a land option, and then re-board for a trip to the true North Pole. The ship would return to Barrow, and the passengers would fly back to Seattle.

"Oh, I'm sorry! I wasn't paying attention. Are you okay?"

Dan had barely felt the bump. "Yes, I'm fine." Brought back to reality, he realized the crowds around him had already grown substantially. The ship only held 120 passengers and 60 officers and crew, but in addition to his fellow travelers, there were now hundreds of well wishers, security, protesters, reporters, and the curious. He looked to see if he recognized anyone and tried to arrange his face into the mask he had seen on the tourists when he worked at Darwin's Research Station in the Galapagos Islands. It was a reverent but ignorant look. Like a pig in church, McGrath used to say. McGrath taught Dan to hate that look, and now he had the chance to wipe it off the face of the earth.

"So are you going on the Swallow too?" The lumpy, balding man bent down to tie his shoe and then picked up the smallest of his three bags which he had dropped when he tripped into Dan. Dan noticed the pipe stem sticking out of his pocket.

"Um, yeah." Dan knew he should say more, but the accidental encounter had taken him by surprise and for some reason made him uneasy. Having spent so much time only with his fellow eco-saviors, as they liked to call themselves, he had forgotten that other people were people up close, not objects or problems. And the pipe reminded him of his father. Spending as much time as possible in his cabin or at least alone would be the key to making this work, he realized. Emily was right.

"The trip of a lifetime, eh? She looks not quite big enough somehow, compared to regular cruise ships. I mean she's tall, that's for sure, but not terribly long. But they say she can cut through 10 feet of ice! Amazing. I just hope the lunatics," the man jerked his head in the direction of the sign waving protestors, "don't slow us down. After what happened last week...."

Dan instantly and with relief lost his nascent empathy for the man. Earth United had been staging protests across the city about so-called eco-travel. Last week, one got out of hand. The stranger shook his head and waited politely and almost eagerly for a response. Feeling the lack of a connection and still juggling his luggage, he gave up and headed awkwardly for the boarding line. "See you on board, I guess," was his parting line.

The encounter, unwelcome and trivial as it was, proved to Dan that he was well disguised. He reminded himself that no one would be looking at him as closely as he was looking at them, unless HALO had hired security on the ship, which he doubted. It would mean losing a paying passenger. Searching in the smaller of his two duffel bags as the crowds grew, Dan pulled out his sunglasses, shook them open and slid them on. That was better. Now he could stare without being obvious. Emily had been worried about all the luggage he would have to take making him stand out, but she needn't have. Everyone seemed to have four or five bags, even though the ship provided the parkas they would need when it got really cold further north, as well as a library and computers in addition to food, entertainment and lectures. For a ticket price that amounted to a year's salary for a scientist, you definitely wouldn't lack for much. His three bags – the two duffels and a backpack – seemed positively spartan in number.

"I am sooooo excited," yelped an older woman to her companion. "Do we have enough batteries for the camera? I hope I didn't forget anything," she continued as they made their way up the ramp. It was hard to tell if the man was her son, husband, nurse, or boyfriend. He looked like he stepped off the cover of GQ and calmly helped her along with a hand on her elbow, a gesture that had the aura of paid caring about it. Behind them was a family of five. Spoiled kids, Dan thought. When he was little, his family was lucky to go camping for a few days at the lake. Then his father died, ending even those meager vacations.

"How can you be cold already? It's sunny and 60 without a bit of wind!" Another conversation floated to him above the general din.

"I'm anticipating cold. We're going all the way to the Arctic Circle for god's sake, because you wanted to. And the ship looks cold and forbidding. I'm going to freeze." A pleasant trip is in store for him, Dan thought.

"The ship isn't cold! It has more power than any other type of ship. It's used to going to ice covered places. That's why they call it an icebreaker. I imagine it can generate enough heat to keep you from being inconvenienced."

The crewman at the top of the plank smiled and assured the arguing couple that the ship could and would provide plenty of warmth. "Those engines do crank out the heat, ma'am, in addition to powering the ship. The closer we get to the Arctic Circle, the colder the outside air will get, but it will still be only early autumn. This ship keeps us warm even on winter trips. You'll be just fine." Angry wife gave him a look, but seemed reassured. The husband's grateful smile made Dan chuckle.

The itinerary called for a brief safety talk before they left port, a longer one that evening at dinner and a lifeboat drill the next morning. Dan would be conducting his own safety drills but looked forward to this one as an opportunity to put the last pieces of the puzzle together. He checked his watch. 10:30. Departure in 90 minutes. Despite the distractions and his efforts at mental discipline, Dan felt a little queasy again. He was disappointed in himself, in the way his emotions were on such a roller coaster and the way the fear could sneak up and get control. He knew a routine would help, and he'd have time on board to develop one. Nothing could happen for at least a week and probably two. It was up to him to determine the best location to execute the plan, and the best location would depend upon the weather and the exact route. The ship would detour to follow any reports of animal sightings.

The herd of tourists continued to board, along with the rest of the crew, one of whom had a dog in a flashy red harness. It looked so out of place, Dan had to fight the urge to run up like a child and ask to pet it. It was a gorgeous animal, too; it looked like a husky or some sort of sled dog. He wondered how a dog could live on a ship and if it had a job or something, then they got swallowed up by the rest of the crowd.

Dan soon forgot about the dog in the sea of faces. They all looked so happy, so excited and guilt-free, but they should look like junkies, Dan thought. Just like addicts, their desires have costs, but they were gifted, probably from birth, with the ability to close their eyes to those costs. If they could afford it, they could see no reason not to have it. He felt the strength of the righteous once again. Fear left him, and even though he knew it was temporary, it was good to be free of it. Hatred was the safe path, his beacon out of the confusing bag of thoughts he always carried. He had to remember there was only one right side and he was on it. It would be lonely for a while, but he would get over it and get down to work. Then when he got back, Earth United could start planning their next project. Although for the first time, Dan realized there had been no talk of a next project.

The ship's horn sounded. "All aboard!"

Dan shouldered his backpack which was heavy from the two guns and twenty pounds of explosives and grabbed the handles of the other two bags. He headed up the ramp as ready for his mission as he could be.

The first day was uneventful and a little disorienting as Dan tried to make a mental map of his surroundings. He woke on his second day at sea, though, to find the ship enshrouded in a magical fog that robbed everything it touched of color, blending the whole world into an ethereal nothingness. It gradually thinned to reveal a glittering silver sky and then evaporated completely by noon. The speed of the transformation was amazing. The sky became a shade of blue he had never seen before, never known existed. It was as if the fog had scrubbed the sky clean. The change in mood and color was so abrupt, it left Dan breathless. He spent the entire day just gazing at the landscape, waiting for something else to happen. The ship was hugging the Queen Charlotte islands which offered views of snow-topped mountains and fjords that plunged into the sea, clouds that hugged the forests and windswept sandy beaches. But the air was the most amazing thing to Dan. It was like breathing light, and it was purer than anything he had ever sucked into his lungs before. It had not entered his mind that he might enjoy the cruise, and he was a little embarrassed. After dinner he enjoyed the music in the bar until he was too tired to keep his eyes open. He would start refocusing on the plan tomorrow, he promised himself as he crawled into bed and fell almost instantly asleep.

Dan was dead to the world when something heavy slammed into the side of his head. The blow woke him up and knocked him senseless at the same time, sending twin waves of shock and panic through his body. Within a couple of seconds the confusion sorted itself out in his brain, and he realized to his horror that he was trapped. The something that hit his head was the wall and another something, probably the bed, was holding it there.

He heard shouts and screams and cracks like gunshots. It was so dark that he couldn't tell if his eyes were open, but he could taste the blood in his mouth. He thought he was also being held down by some deranged attacker and tried to swing his arms in an effort to fight back until he understood that he was alone. He forced himself to calm his breathing so he wouldn't pass out. He heard water rushing into his cabin through what must be his open door. Why was his door open? Then he also realized he was upside down. Something had flipped the ship on its side, Dan realized. Holy shit. But he hadn't done anything yet. It wasn't supposed to happen this way. This wasn't the plan. He remembered the explosives in his bag. Shit. Would they? With the water? He couldn't remember, but he needed to get out. Get away. His head hurt so bad, though, and the pain made him nauseous. Blood ran into his eyes blinding him and increasing his panic. He blinked his eyes clean. He could hear more shouts and screams and splashing. Then an explosion. Waves of freezing water crashed over him until he was completely submerged.

He wasn't a good swimmer, but he was strong and young and he wasn't as injured as he thought he was. Adrenaline helped too. He pushed against the bed until he made a space he could slip through. Then he kicked and kicked and kicked until he was free of the sheets that snaked around his body. He was naked which made it easier to swim once he was free. But he almost couldn't tell the difference between water and air; both were so cold and foreign. He was terrified of sucking water into his lungs so he held his breath as long as he could before risking opening his mouth. The icy water and the lack of air sent him to a mental and physical place he had never been. He thought he was going to die. But then he popped into an air pocket and took huge, gulping breaths until his heart stopped thundering in his chest. Now he felt the cold much more severely. It was as if the water was eating its way through his body.

The problem was he couldn't remember where he was in the ship, or which way was up. In the water, there was no floor, no gravity. Think, damnit. But he couldn't. He heard some more distant shouting, but he could barely help himself, much less anyone else. And he couldn't even tell where the sounds were coming from. He couldn't see anything. So he took a deep breath and dove under, feeling for a way out. Hard objects slammed into him. He started to pray, but he kept moving. He collided with softer things which felt like other people, already dead. He squealed in panic and horror but kept swimming and pushing when he ran into things. It was his only option.

Then with a rush that felt like a trip down a water slide at Six Flags, he was free of the ship and out in the open water. He tilted his head back and bobbed in the choppy water for a moment, amazed to be free. His legs were starting to go numb, though, and he could feel the heavy water squeezing the life out of him, as if it were alive. He heard more screams, but not as many as before. Then came the terrifying sound of the ship breaking apart. His eardrums reverberated with the power of the noise. Flames burst from the center of the ship, where she had split in two. It was unreal. The fire, thank god, made it possible to see a little. He swam as close as he could around the edge of the listing pieces of the ship to try and find a lifeboat. Or something to climb on before he froze to death. But there was nothing where the lifeboats were supposed to be. Or where he thought they were supposed to be. Shit, he didn't know anything.

Just as Dan realized it was raining, lightning illuminated a swath of red at the periphery of his vision. It was a kayak, and it was far away from the boat, as if it had been shot from a cannon. He swam for it as best he could; with his limbs frozen and his heart racing, he couldn't get through the water quickly enough. And the waves were huge, misdirecting things that seemed to want to fight him for the kayak. Lightning helped him continue to get glimpses of the red, but it seemed like with each flash the kayak had jumped to a new location. He made himself be ready for the next wave. Holding his breath, Dan dove as deeply as he could until the power of the wave was above him. He almost didn't feel the cold anymore. He could set his own course down here, out of the reach of the wave's curling force, if only he could remember which way was up. Tunneling first toward where he last saw the kayak and then toward the surface, Dan found salvation when his head hit something hard. It was the kayak. He hugged it; it was narrow enough at the end that he could get his arms all the way around it. This wouldn't do much good, though, he thought. I'll freeze in this water. I have to get out. He slid his arms up the body of the boat and frog kicked his legs. He was terrified of having the boat ripped from him by the next wave. He stopped his sliding when he got near the middle and felt for the cockpit. It had a cover that was still attached so the little boat hadn't taken on water. Dan fumbled with his useless hands and finally ripped it off with a burst of energy and worked to haul himself inside.

Halfway in, Dan felt something bump his legs. A panicked scream shot from his gut and he kicked his way out of the water with the speed of someone about to be eaten. Once on the boat, the next flash of lightning showed Dan the pale, almost glowing fur of a dog. Then blackness. Then more lightning seared a snapshot of the dog's panicked blue eyes into his own eyes. Dan could not leave the dog to die, not the way it looked at him. At the risk of tipping the kayak and filling it with water, Dan reached his arm into the water and around the struggling dog's body to lift it in. The dog's claws dug into him as its feet searched for solid ground. Dan yelled in pain and shifted to the side as he used all the strength he had left in his back to heave her up and nearly tipped the boat. The dog slipped down to Dan's feet and seemed relieved to stay there in its makeshift cave, quivering with fear and cold.

Once in, Dan realized that this was the wooden kayak he had seen on the ship on his first day's wanderings, the one the crewman told him was designed to carry him and his dog, Scout. This had to be Scout. Dan tried not to think of the man searching for his dog. The dog must have a sixth sense or something to be able to find the boat in all this chaos. He couldn't believe their luck. Somehow, Dan knew that their escape depended on their honoring that luck by staying together. He started to shiver violently and wrapped as much of himself as he could around the dog's body and huddled with it in the cockpit. Almost immediately, the arctic dawn started teasing its way through the clouds.

The remnants of the storm seemed to slink away with the night. He knew storms could come up quickly in the Arctic, but this was crazy. And the waves he swam through, while huge to him, couldn't have sunk a ship. There must have been a rogue wave. Dan had never experienced one, but he'd read about them. There is nothing you can do when they hit.

He un-kinked his body and started opening hatches using his teeth and the sides of his palms because his fingers were nearly useless. He desperately needed something to wear. The dog had kept him from freezing for however long they were wrapped around each other – Dan figured it couldn't have been more than an hour - but just barely, and he needed insulation in the form of clothes. It was a two-person kayak he remembered, and he turned and saw the second cockpit behind him. He struggled to pull the cover off of it and saw it was smaller and shallower. This must be where the dog normally sits, he thought. He shook his head at the ingenuity of the design. It was a lovely and large boat. He continued searching the other spaces while his teeth chattered so fiercely he thought they would break off and finally found a survival suit and some other clothes as well as food and water, gloves, a pair of neoprene boots, a few medical supplies, a pack of hand warmers, two space blankets and a tent. He activated two handwarmers and clutched them until his fingers thawed, an extraordinarily painful process. But afterwards, he could pull on the long underwear and pants and a jacket and tug on the gloves and huge boots. He stuffed the spray skirt down by his legs. He had stopped bleeding, but when he pulled on the wool hat, it made him yelp with pain. He had a large scrape on his scalp; it wasn't deep, but it hurt.

Scout hadn't moved, and Dan was painfully grateful for the dog's presence. He reached for the sides of the boat and found two paddles still lashed there. He slid one out and started paddling just to generate some heat, although the sun was surprisingly warm. The ship was gone, as far as Dan could tell. And he hadn't heard any other screams in a long time. The silence was creepy. How could he be the only one alive? It wasn't supposed to be like this. He was going to hijack the ship and make everyone go ashore. Then he was going to set the explosives and sink the ship from the safety of a Zodiac. He would zoom away until he was out of sight and then radio Randy and Emily. Then they would pick him up and . . . Dan realized he never knew what was supposed to happen to the passengers. How could he have been so stupid? On land, though, they would have stood a chance. They would have been rescued. Now they were all dead thanks to some kind of crazy storm. The thought that he had wanted all these people to die made him sick. He couldn't remember feeling strong enough to destroy anything.

The sun finished rising and put an end to the dark part of the nightmare. But the beginning of this phase didn't seem much better. Dan knew the presence of full daylight ignited hope like little else, but he also knew that hope was a very unstable emotion. The storm had vanished as quickly as it came leaving no trace. The water was so smooth, silky even, that it seemed impossible it had ever gathered itself into a violent, killing wave. The sun was soon bright and high enough that without wind, Dan was starting to warm up. He pointed himself toward what he thought was east, where the sky was brightest and land should be, and paddled.

The sky and water were so blue, they seemed to merge into one thing. And they might as well be, Dan thought. He stopped paddling and clipped the paddle onto the deck. Hearing the sound, Scout crawled out from Dan's feet and poked its head up. The dog finished pulling itself out of the cockpit and stood on the deck. She was apparently a she. She walked carefully to the bow and relieved herself, then settled into an indentation on the deck that looked carved out just for her, and curled into a ball to watch Dan. She seemed to be trying to figure out her situation and sizing Dan up, deciding whether she could follow this new human master or whether she would have to lead.

He resumed paddling, but his arms quickly grew tired, so he had to take frequent breaks. But every time he stopped, the horror of his situation threatened to overtake him. Blue, cold water was all he saw. Unless he looked at Scout. Thank god she found him. I mean Jesus Christ Dan thought, I could go crazy out here alone. And she really was beautiful. A cream and rust colored Siberian Husky. He had only seen them on television before, although a few people had the black and white variety in Seattle. Scout looked back at him in a way he couldn't understand, but it was calming. Her look seemed to say: "It's just you and me. We'll figure it out." The dog also seemed to be asking him for something. Although Dan thought the only way he would survive is if the dog helped him.

He shifted his mind to the mathematical problem of rationing the food and water. There were six bottles of water and two metal tins of packaged granola bar-type things. The label on the tins was in Russian. Dan opened one of the packages and tried a bite and nearly spit it out it was so terrible. Choking the rest down, he told himself eating was the key to both having the strength to find land and not going crazy along the way. He gave a few chunks to the dog and the first bar was gone in seconds. He saw there were 23 of whatever that was left. The scientist in him came alive. "One a day" he thought. That is all we can do. "Are you with me?" he asked his companion. Scout continued to watch him with a gaze filled with both servitude and power that seemed to say maybe. Her thoughtful response both unnerved and ennobled him.

He drank a sip of water and dumped the rest of the bars from one tin into his pockets and poured some water in the tin for Scout. She lapped it carefully, as if she knew it was precious. Or maybe she was always so deliberate and contained in her movements. Dan didn't know much about dogs; he had never had a pet of any kind.

He resumed paddling but stopped when Scout leapt up and started barking. The kayaked rocked wildly. He steadied the craft and looked where she was looking and saw huge black shapes breaking the water. Orcas. Scout stopped barking once she saw Dan notice the whales and looked at him, then sat down to continue watching the whales. She had done her job of sounding the alarm. Dan counted ten or twelve. He couldn't be totally sure. They seemed to weave in and out of each other. They were moving perpendicular to the kayak's path, which Dan decided meant that he and Scout were headed in the right direction. The giant animals were lovely and frightening at the same time. He felt a strange stab of jealousy; unlike Dan and Scout, they were at home.

Dan made himself stop thinking about them and settled into working on the mental calculations needed to fine tune a course for land, their only chance for rescue, he figured. Rescue. What would that mean? Who would come? Would they know what Dan and Earth United had been planning? What were the news reports saying? It was all too much to imagine. Anyway, he was getting hot from the sun and the effort of paddling. He unzipped his jacket and stuck a hand in the icy ocean and splashed the water on his face and head. Then he scooped some over Scout's back and rubbed it in. Scout seemed to enjoy it. He stretched a little, and started the rhythmic strokes he hoped and feared would bring them out of this beautiful hell. What would happen when he got back? Would Randy and Emily be upset? Would anyone be there?

He paddled until his arms were numb and decided to lay down for a minute. It was awkward, and he had to arch his back, but it felt good. Scout settled into her place on the deck. Dan hoped they would not drift too far. He closed his eyes and somehow fell asleep. He woke with a start in the dark, with his back in unbelievable pain. It must be hours later, he realized. His mouth was so dry and again he couldn't tell if his eyes were open or closed. Then the moon came out from behind a cloud, and one by one the stars winked at him. It was beautiful and bright enough to be daytime, but he had no strength anymore to paddle. How long could he survive he wondered? A day, three, a week, more? He didn't know. He almost didn't care. He was so tired, so confused. Despair was waiting on the edges of his mind, ready to jump in and take over.

"I just need another day to pull myself together. Then I'll figure something out for us," he said to Scout. He hoped he had a day. More bad weather could come, or he could lose his shit entirely, he realized. Anything could happen out here in a split second. In fact he had more than a day. Four days passed with paddling, talking to Scout, and one bar and three sips of water per day. She spent the days alternating positions between her cockpit and the deck, but she tucked in at Dan's feet for the nights. It was comforting. His hips were cramping, though, and his hands were blistered. He knew he was getting severely dehydrated and that Scout was too. Her eyes were looking sunken and her fur was matted. They both smelled bad. He tried to keep his body cool with seawater during the days so he wouldn't sweat out too much of his body's precious water. The nights were cold, but short, thanks to the long days of late summer. Dan tried to think of Emily and Randy and his other colleagues, but they were little dots on the edges of his memory. He wondered where the drift was taking them.

On the fifth day, Dan and Scout had their regular breakfast: half a granola bar and a sip of water. He had learned to paddle sitting on the deck of the kayak with his feet in the cockpit. The different position helped his body, and he was feeling good about their ability to survive for a least a little while longer. All of a sudden, he heard a whooshing sound and looked up as the sky went dark with birds that seemed to appear from nowhere. They filled the sky all the way down to the horizon, and their noise quickly became deafening. Scout was up and barking at them the way she did at the Orcas. Maybe it means we're close to land, Dan hoped. He looked in the direction the birds had come from and thought he saw something. Once Scout was finished looking at where the birds went, she looked in the direction of Dan's gaze and wagged her tail. That must be land, Dan thought with a spike of joy. He picked up the paddle and put all he had into moving the kayak toward land.

The tide was going in so they got a push from the last wave that sent the kayak halfway up the beach. Scout jumped off immediately and did donuts on the gravelly beach, like a teenager in a dunebuggy. Dan pulled the kayak past the high water mark and looked around. To mark the occasion, he decided to break his one bar a day rule and gave Scout two of her own and ate one by himself. Scout snatched the bars as if they were alive and swallowed them, then scampered away with delight and cocked her leg on everything around them. Dan had never seen a female dog lift her leg, and he shook his head. Maybe it was the breed. No pee came out of course since she was so dehydrated, but she was unfazed by this hiccup.

Dan pulled the supplies off of the kayak and started worrying about wildlife. They were safe on the kayak, he realized. He had no weapons other than Scout, and he knew he would die if something happened to her. She was all he had. Finished with her rounds, she returned and nudged Dan's hand. She rolled over on her back and presented her belly for rubbing. Land apparently made everything okay for Scout; Dan wished he could feel half her glee. He set up the tent as best he could and pulled out the survival suit for Scout to nest in. Not to be moving, not to be on that impossibly blue water that had looked so lovely from the ship but so deadly from the kayak, was wonderful. They fell asleep, but Dan was soon awakened by the cold. The seasons seemed to have changed overnight. Scout was less affected by the temperature drop, but even she was shivering a little until she had her morning romp. He chased her and played fetch until he felt warmer, too. Afterwards, they had a bar each and some water, but before they had even digested their breakfast, the weather got worse. The sun that had greeted them had left in a hurry, and it was snowing. Dan crawled back into the tent and tried to think. Maybe they should head inland tomorrow and look for a road or something. He put his head in his hands and rubbed his temples.

He heard it before he saw it. The low rumble of an old, overworked engine. Scout heard it too and started barking. He stood up and screamed at the top of his lungs and jumped up and down until he was too out of breath to scream anymore. Panicked that they would miss their only chance, he ran to the kayak and stood it on end and then waved the paddle. Then he beat the paddle against the hull to make more noise. The boat was still coming, wasn't it? He couldn't tell by sound or by sight. He started throwing rocks into the water. Then in a flash, he realized his stupidity and grabbed Scout and tossed her in the kayak. They pushed off and he tried to sprint to the boat. The sudden effort released so much lactate into his muscles that they started to freeze up. His chest burned and he gasped for breath. But he just dug in harder, tried to pull more water with each stroke of the paddle. He screamed; Scout barked. Finally, when he thought he had used his last ounce of energy, a horn sounded, and he knew they were spotted. He stopped paddling and lay back, utterly exhausted and relieved. Scout stood on the prow and wagged her tail. He didn't think to wonder who might be on the boat.

It seemed to take forever for the boat to reach them, and when it did, she cut her engines.

"I saw you on the shore. Sorry we didn't hit the horn sooner. You didn't have to come all the way out here," said a short, square person who looked like a man but sounded like a woman.

"I . . . I didn't know. I can't believe this is really happening. I am so glad to see you."

"I bet you are. Hold on, we'll lower the sled and you and your dog can hop on. Rupert will get your kayak. Do you need anything from shore? Seeing as you left in such a hurry."

It was like being rescued by the Ritz Carlton, Dan thought, grateful for his rescuer's kindness and competence.

"No. Nothing," he finally answered.

"No mementos, huh? Okey dokey, then."

When they were all on board, Dan quickly got new clothes and a milky sweet concoction that the woman, her gender being obvious once she took her hat off, made him drink. Scout got chicken scraps which she devoured and a cup of water.

"No more water for you until we're sure that stays down, okay girl?"

Scout looked up and telegraphed her assent with a ferociously wagging tail. She was clearly home.

"Dinner for humans is in an hour. My name is Captain Anne, and at dinner, you can tell me how you survived out there in a kayak with a dog."

Dan nodded.

"You don't speak much, do you?"

"I'm a little shell shocked."

"That is completely understandable. You can bunk there with Rupert. He likes dogs. See you in an hour." Captain Anne pointed down the hall to a room with two bunks, a desk, and not much else.

Dan sat on the bottom bunk and Scout hopped up next to him. He didn't know what the world knew about the Arctic Swallow. It had been what, six days, since she sank. Had Earth United done anything? Claimed credit? Were there any other survivors? Just because he didn't see any . . . Dan needed to know what other people knew and were saying. Scout rolled onto her back and exposed her belly for the second time since he'd known her, so Dan rubbed it and tried to think.

A bell rang and roused Dan from his worrying before he'd settled anything in his head. He figured it meant dinner, so he splashed water on his face and smoothed his hair and stepped into the tiny hall. Food would help.

"Follow me. I'm Rupert," said a red haired man who looked like the dictionary definition of an ancient Viking explorer.

"I'm Dan. Thanks."

"Usually we're a lot busier than this, but this is a strange trip. You're lucky, because if it was a regular trip, we would never have been this far west and able to hunt for survivors. It's been some real strange weather lately."

Survivors? So word was out? Dan felt caught, but figured he should just play along. "Where was I?"

"St. Matthew Island. In the technical middle of fucking nowhere." Rupert most certainly did not have a Viking accent. He sounded vaguely Texan.

"Were there any others?"

"None that we found and none that we heard of. You're it. You're lucky."

"I guess so."

"Yup. You're still discombobulated, aren't you? I was stranded at sea once after a shipwreck for a week. Not up here, though. Still, it messes with your mind. You'll be okay in a while." Rupert grinned. "Come on."

Scout led the way, and Dan swore she was grinning, too.

They ate in the kitchen, nine people and a dog around a table sized for six. But the food was plentiful and smelled great. After everyone had served themselves, Anne said a simple grace.

"Dear Lord, thank you for another safe day on the water."

"Amen," everyone answered.

"So how the hell did you manage to luck into that fancy boat and that dog? You're from the Arctic Swallow, right?" Anne said all that with a mouthful of mashed potatoes.

Dan nodded.

"Figured. We heard on the radio that contact with the ship had been lost, but there was no SOS. Coast Guard asked all of us out here to keep an eye out. I've been hit by a rogue wave before, so I figured that's what it was, especially considering that crazy waves had been hitting the cove. What happened exactly?"

Dan told them as best he could, leaving out the bit about how he was supposed to sink the ship.

"You must have been scared out of your mind. First time on a cruise like that?"

"Yes, but I've been on research ships in the Pacific."

"Ah, that's nothing like the Bering Sea. The Bering Sea is a nasty old bitch, but I love her. I'm 58 years old, and I finally feel like I can read her. I've been fishing my whole life and captain of my own ship for 22 years. She's cold and rough and can change in a flash. But nothing, nothing is as real. But I guess you know that or you wouldn't have gone on that trip."

Dan said nothing. He didn't know what to say.

"Ah, Captain's just a sentimental old coot," said Rupert with a wink. "I bet you're done with the sea for while, eh, Dan?"

"Old coot? That is mutiny, or at least insubordination. You're doing dishes," said Anne, laughing.

Scout made rounds as everyone ate and introduced themselves and told tales of big waves and bigger fish. Anne got up when most of the food was eaten. "I guess this qualifies as a special occasion, at least for you, huh Dan?" Anne pulled the stopper out of a bottle of scotch and everyone drained their water glass and held it out for a splash of the rationed liquor.

"Cheers, everyone." Anne drank hers in one sip. "But just because we've done our good deed today doesn't mean we get sloppy on chores, right?"

Everyone groaned and grumbled but got up and divided into pairs to clear the table, do the dishes, take care of the trash, and clean the floor.

After chores, everyone went their separate ways. Dan and Scout headed up to the deck where they found Captain Anne. He stood what he hoped was a respectful distance away, about five feet, and leaned against the railing.

"You have a story, don't you? I can see it in your eyes. And don't lie. I don't care what it is so long as I and my crew are not in danger. Are we?"

It just started to snow. This time, it was lovely.

"No," Dan said.

"Good enough. We'll hit port in about a week. Think you can manage that long with us? I'll have to assign you some chores or the crew will get resentful."

"That's fine with me. You've been wonderful."

"It's just how you treat shipwreck survivors. And fellow wanderers. People think fishermen up here are crazy drunk fools, and we are, but we're good people too. The best, I'd say."

"So far, I'd have to agree."

Captain Anne snorted. "You ain't got much to choose form right now."

"Look, can we stay on? I figured if you have an empty bunk, you're short one man."

"Are you asking for a job? Now, why would a man who can afford a cruise that costs a heap more than my new truck need a job like this?"

Dan didn't answer. Anne just looked at him for a while, as if reading his face.

"You probably could get a share of some settlement or insurance or something. Get a lawyer and cash in."

"I don't think I want to do that," Dan said.

Anne dug around in her pockets for a while and waited for her mind to make itself up.

"Okay, I'll give you a shot, but only because I like your dog and she seems to like you. Animals have good sense. The minute you do anything I don't like, though, I'll put you out on the sea in that kayak you came in on, and I'm keeping the dog. My terms, take it or leave it. Deal?"

"Deal," Dan said without hesitation, and they shook on it.

###

ABOUT THE AUTHOR

"Writing for me feels like carving an intricate, tiny wood sculpture, except that I have to grow the tree before I can start. So I plant the seed, water and fertilize and nurture it, weed the area around it, provide mulch, protect it from storms, prune dead limbs, and do everything I can to help it grow big and strong. Then I have to chop it down, peel off the bark, cut it into manageable sections, haul a section inside to the workroom, study it, put on safety glasses, turn on a bright light, gather tools and start carving. Following the grain of the wood and taking the time to find out what the tree wanted to be, I eventually transform the hunk of green wood into something so different, only the tree and I know it came from the original seed."

Laura Semonche Jones is a North Carolina native currently living with her husband and their animals (two pit bull mixes and two agile and tolerant cats) in Charlottesville, Virginia. She thinks she published her first piece of fiction in *Cricket Magazine* when she was twelve-ish, but she can't find the clipping to prove it to you.

A double graduate of the University of North Carolina at Chapel Hill, Laura practiced law for ten years and co-owned an art gallery for three before starting to write professionally seven years ago. When not writing, reading, or thinking about fiction, Laura works as a freelance writer and editor, enjoys open water swimming and dreams of the day when dogs can talk. *Breaking and Entering* is her first collection of short stories. She is now working on a mystery novel, *Picking Up Mercury*, about how a reluctant female sleuth and former swimmer navigates the unmarked intersection of journalism and justice where it is easy to lose one's innocence, and easier to die.

She maintains a website at www.LauraSJones.com.

Made in the USA
Charleston, SC
13 November 2011